THE MIDNIGHT SECRET

RITE WORLD: LIGHTGROVE WITCHES
BOOK 4

JULIANA HAYGERT

COPYRIGHT

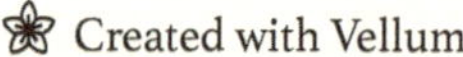 Created with Vellum

RITE WORLD

Welcome to the RITE WORLD!

For a printable reading order, click here!

Free Novellas:
The Vampire Hunt
The Light Witch

Novellas:
The Hunter Path
The Light Calling
The Light Witch
The Wicked Alliance
The Shadow Fae

Rite World:
The Vampire Heir (Book 1)
The Witch Queen (Book 2)
The Immortal Vow (Book 3)
The Warlock Lord (Book 4)
The Wolf Consort (Book 5)
The Crystal Rose (Book 6)
The Wolf Forsaken (Book 7)
The Fae Bound (Book 8)
The Blood Pact (Book 9)

Rite World: Blackthorn Hunters Academy
The Demons Kiss (Book 1)
The Hunter Secret (Book 2)
The Soul Bond (Book 3)
The Shadow Trials (Book 4)
The Immortal Vow (Book 5)

Rite World: Vampire Wars
The Darkest Vampire (Book 1)
The Darkest Witch (Book 2)
The Darkest Magic (Book 3)

Rite World: Night Wolves
The Night Calling (Book 1)
The Night Burning (Book 2)
The Night Hunting (Book 3)
The Night Rising (Book 4)

Rite World: Lightgrove Witches

The Midnight Test (Book 1)
The Midnight Spell (Book 2)
The Midnight Flame (Book 3)
The Midnight Secret (Book 4)
The Midnight Hunt (Book 5)

And more to come!

AUTHOR'S NOTE

I hope you enjoy reading *The Midnight Secret*!

Don't forget to sign up for my Newsletter to find out about new releases, cover reveals, giveaways, and more!

If you want to see exclusive teasers, help me decide on covers, read excerpts, talk about books, etc, join my reader group on Facebook: Juliana's Club!

1

I DIDN'T SLEEP AFTER THAT. HOW COULD I? NO, INSTEAD, I texted Sean, but of course, at three in the morning, he was fast asleep.

I paced my bedroom, the panic barely contained, and tried to think.

All right, what did I know so far?

1) The Brotherhood was up to something. I had seen them at Towland. They had captured me, thinking I knew where Arianna's grimoire, necklace, and ashes were.

2) Arianna's familiar, Shade, had helped Sean save me from the Brotherhood. He said I couldn't trust anyone and that he would be back.

I snorted. He wouldn't come here to talk to me, and ... why me? Couldn't he choose a more powerful witch?

And that lead to:

3) The magic around my magic, keeping it contained. No one else but Moira and I knew about it, at least not in this castle. She had told me to not tell anyone about it, and

I had done what she said. Why? It wasn't like I trusted the woman. Perhaps I should tell someone. The council, the queen. If they knew, maybe they could help me.

Or not, since now:

4) The queen and the council thought I had aided the dark witch in escaping the dungeon, and because of that, I was a prisoner in my bedroom.

I wondered if they had caught her. Imprisoned her again. Killed her.

And let's not forget about:

5) The dark lightning. I had seen it a total of three times, but there could have been more that I didn't know about. And there were the runes. Each time, I had seen a different rune.

I sat down at my desk and drew the latest rune alongside the others in my notes. With everything else happening, I had long since abandoned my research, but maybe now was the time to find the underlying cause of this.

I turned the page and jotted down quick notes about everything happening and then stared at it, trying to see some connection between it all. There had to be. If there wasn't anything between all the five items, then at least two or three. It couldn't all be a coincidence.

Early morning, breakfast was brought to me. Rodd wasn't at my door anymore, but two other Light Order warriors were. I asked them if the dark witch had been captured but they didn't answer me.

I was munching on my bagel with cream cheese when my phone rang.

"Hi," I said, dejected.

"What the fuck happened?" Sean sounded furious.

Well, I had sent a text to him at three in the morning saying I had become a prisoner.

I told him what I knew so far, and I also told him about my notes. "I'm trying to see where they all link together."

"There might be no link between them all."

"I know, but I'm here, without anything to do, sleep-deprived, without any news, and my mind is way too active."

Sean sighed. "Maybe if I could see those notes. I'm a visual guy."

My heart squeezed. "I can take a picture of the pages and send them to you."

"That would work."

I quickly took pictures of my notes and sent them to him. "You can look at them later, when you're not busy. No rush."

"Of course we're in a rush, we need to figure this out quick." He paused. "I'm supposed to move there tomorrow. Maybe I can talk to Fynn, and he'll let me come today, then I can talk to you face-to-face."

"No one is talking to me, not even the Light Order warriors guarding my door."

"Shit, that's insane. You're not dangerous!"

"I feel like I should take that as an insult."

He chuckled. "I meant you're not evil. I bet you can be dangerous when you want."

A small smile adorned my lips. "That's better." A knock came from my door, and I stood at attention. A second later, the door opened, and Moira stepped inside. "Sean, Moira is here. I'll call you later."

I didn't wait to hear his answer. I turned off the call and faced Moira.

She looked around at my room, then finally her eyes settled on me. I had changed from my pajamas to leggings and a comfy sweater, but I was barefoot, and had no makeup on. Her gaze shifted to the desk behind me, where all my notes and drawings were spread out in plain sight.

Shit.

Thankfully, she returned her eyes to mine. "How are you?"

I scoffed. "Are you serious?"

She nodded. "I thought you would like to know the witch is still at large and the Light Order and the elite witches are out looking for her."

I crossed my arms. "Why are you telling me this? Do you also think I helped her and you're trying to get something from me? Newsflash: I didn't help her. I have no idea why she came to see me before escaping." I still couldn't shake how terrifying it had been to wake up with her on top of me. "I don't know how to prove my innocence."

"I don't know if you can."

I balked. "W-what?"

She let out a long breath. "Hazel, it's dangerous right now. I'm working on a way of getting you out of here. And—"

I took a step back. "Getting me out of here?"

"Yes. You can't stay here. We need to—"

"You're asking me to run as if I were a criminal? I won't do that!"

"I know you're not a criminal, but if you stay here—"

"Do you even hear yourself?" I was appalled. I never expected this from Moira. "And even if it made sense, I wouldn't go with you. I don't trust you!"

Moira glared at me, her fists clenched. "You don't have a choice!"

"Excuse me? If I say I won't go, I won't go!"

She groaned. "Hazel ... something is going on, something big, and we need to act before it happens."

"What?"

"I don't know, not everything, I can't—" She clamped her lips, shaking her head once. "It doesn't matter. As your mentor, it's my duty to make sure you're safe and the only way for you to be safe is to get out of here as soon as possible."

"You never wanted to be my mentor. You have detested me since the moment I set foot in this castle. I really doubt you want me to be safe."

"By the light." Moira ran a hand down her face. "I won't argue anymore, Hazel. Prepare a small bag. When I come back, we're leaving. Be ready."

I opened my mouth to tell her no but decided against it. The woman sounded crazy, so I let her go on with her delusion. It seemed she wouldn't take no for an answer, so I let her believe I would comply. The next time she came, I would yell for the guards outside my door.

She marched out of my bedroom as fast as she had

come in, and I sat down at my desk, still shaken by the brief exchange.

There was one thing I knew: If I ran, then the council would assume I was guilty. The Light Order would hunt me, and things would only go downhill from there.

I wasn't willing to follow that path.

I DIDN'T KNOW WHAT TO DO WITH MYSELF. BEING IN MY room, with only my phone to text Sean, was boring as hell. I paced around the room, I stared out the window at the endless green landscape behind the castle, I lay in bed and tried to nap.

At noon, I was brought lunch, and then in the middle of the afternoon, I was brought a snack. Again, the Light Order guards handed me things and didn't talk to me or answer my questions. I didn't see Rodd or Fynn anymore, and no one else came to see me.

When the sun started its slow descent beyond the horizon, I stared at my phone. My internet had been disconnected as soon as they told me I was in lockdown, so I couldn't watch Netflix or browse social media. But I could still text and call. I had been texting Sean here and there. He had told me he called Fynn, but they weren't answering him either, and when he tried coming into the castle through the antique store, he was told he had to wait until tomorrow.

I could call my mother. Did she know what was going on here? That the coven she idolized so much was keeping her daughter prisoner? If she knew, she would have called me already, wouldn't she? And if she didn't know, then I wouldn't be the one to tell her. I didn't want to worry her.

But I wanted to hear her voice.

"Hazel!" she answered with a chirpy tone after two rings. "How are you doing, sweetie?"

"Hey, Mom. I'm ... good. How are you?"

"I'm fine. I'm fine. I was about to start dinner. Your sister is out with a friend, and I'm all by myself. Why don't you tell me how things are going while I cook? I bet it's wonderful and I want to hear all about it."

I suppressed a sigh. I didn't want her to know how frustrated I was, and for some reason, I hated shattering the image she had of the Lightgrove coven.

"Everything is great," I lied, feeling like the worst daughter ever. I spun things around, embellishing them a little—all right, a lot. I even told her about Sean, but I lied he was already in the Light Order and we had met here.

A hole would appear under my feet and hell would swallow me whole at any second.

"They are calling us for dinner, Mom," I lied again. "I have to go."

"Of course, sweetie. Have a great night."

"You too."

I hung up and my sadness and despair only grew. What the hell was I doing?

And how would I fix this mega problem I was in if I couldn't speak with anyone?

Like an answer to my prayers, a knock came from the

door and Grace's head popped in. "Hi, there. May I come in?"

I almost rolled my eyes at her. "Of course."

She stepped into the room and closed the door behind her. Her snake was nowhere in sight. "I wanted to see how you're doing?"

A lump rose in my throat and my eyes misted over. "Not so great."

She nodded, walked over to me, and gave me a hug. "I'm so sorry about this mess, my dear." She pulled back but didn't let go of my hands. "As you can imagine, things are crazy right now. We haven't captured the witch yet and—"

"I didn't help her escape!" I blurted out. "I ... I went to see her, but she was so well protected. I asked a few questions, she didn't answer, and I walked away. That was it. Why she asked for me yesterday and how she escaped, I have no idea."

She squeezed my hands. "I know, my dear. I believe you. The council wants to believe you too. Most of us vouch for you, but I'm afraid until we capture the witch or find concrete proof otherwise, you'll remain in this room ... I'm so sorry."

I blinked, pushing the tears away. "Right now, I'm glad you believe in me, and that you're on my side."

"I'm sure we'll figure something soon and you'll be let out. You know what? I'll talk to the council. We'll arrange a better place for you to stay while you wait. Maybe a suite with a living room, a TV, and even a kitchen so you can cook something for yourself if you want. Does that sound good?"

It wasn't what I wanted, but it was better than nothing. "It does."

She gave one last squeeze of my hands then let them go. "Then hang on for now. Dinner will be here soon. Hopefully before bedtime, I'll come to get you and take you to better accommodations."

"Thanks."

"My pleasure, dear." She offered a smile before leaving my bedroom.

I sat on my bed, a little relieved. If Grace, a council member, was on my side, things would be okay. Everything would work out.

2

I ate not even half of my dinner, and texted Sean, who was as frustrated as I was. Night came, and Grace hadn't come back. I lay down on my bed, my mind reeling, my body restless.

What was I supposed to do now? Sleep? I wasn't tired, and I couldn't relax.

Suddenly, the sound of the door clicking woke me up. I glanced to the window. It was pitch black out and faint moonlight streamed past the open curtains.

"What the ...?" I rubbed at my eyes.

Grace stepped out from the darkness, her green snake coiled around her arms and shoulders. "Hazel."

I swallowed a scream and pressed a hand to my chest. "Holy sh—" I forced myself to not curse in front of a council member. "You scared me."

"Sorry." She smiled at me. "I didn't mean to startle you. I could have waited until tomorrow morning to move you, but I thought you were anxious to leave."

"You mean, move to better accommodations?" There was nothing wrong with my room, but I sure could use a TV right now. "I'm ready." Thankfully, I had fallen asleep in my clothes, not my pajamas.

"Let's get a couple of your things." She grabbed my tote from the chair and started shoving my grimoire and notebooks in it. "We'll send someone to pick up the rest later."

"Okay."

I turned on the bedside lamp, so I could see where I was going. I might have some magic in my veins, but I could not see in the dark. Then, I followed her lead, grabbed a small duffel bag from my closet and selected a change of clothes for tomorrow, then in my bathroom. I picked up my toothbrush, toothpaste, hairbrush, and other cosmetics I liked to use every day. I didn't mind staying without the rest for a couple of days. I groaned on the inside. Hopefully, it wouldn't take that long to solve this mess and I would be free of house arrest soon.

Grace hitched my tote over her shoulder, the snake moving to accommodate the strap, and glanced at me. "All done?"

I patted the duffel bag hanging by my side. "Yup."

"Then let's go."

Slowly, she opened the door and spied out. The hallway was eerily dark and there were no guards outside my door. I frowned. "Where are—?"

Grace put a finger to her lips. "Don't speak," she whispered. I could barely hear her. "It's late and we don't want to wake anyone."

Oh-kay.

I followed as Grace walked down the corridor, almost tiptoeing. At every corner, she stopped and looked out before proceeding.

What was going on?

I shook my head. Nope. Whatever that dark thought was, I stopped it right there. Grace was a high-ranked witch, a council member, and she had been nothing but kind and helpful. I trusted her.

On the first floor, Grace led me through a narrow corridor. "Where are we going?" I asked in a whisper. Where was this freaking room? Outside the castle?

"We're almost there," was all she said.

I inhaled deeply and my steps faltered when we crossed a doorway and stepped outside the castle. "Wait ... what's going on?"

Grace wrapped her hand around my wrist. "No time to argue, Hazel. We need to go."

I yanked my arm back. "Not until you tell me what's going on!"

She didn't let go of my wrist. "You insolent—" She inhaled sharply. A dozen Light Order members raced from the side of the castle to us. She glared at me. "We could have been gone by now!"

She extended her free arm and green sparks flew from her palm to the Light Order warriors. Some moved out of the way, others brandished their weapons, deflecting the blows, but still, they slowed down.

"What the hell?" I pulled my arm harder and finally she let go. "Are you insane?"

"For goodness' sake," she muttered. With both hands,

Grace sent a green wave of magic toward the Light Order members. The wave kept coming, unrelenting. The warriors had trouble breaking through it.

"What the hell are you doing?" I started toward the warriors, not sure what I could do.

"You idiot girl." Grace clasped her hand around my upper arm, her grip firm, and a jolt of shock traveled up my arm. I yelped as my body shook and my vision blackened. "Come."

Dazed and numb, I barely registered as Grace dragged me to the nearest portal, through it, and into empty, dark streets.

After several minutes, when we finally turned into a wide alley, the shock's effect wore off.

Six dark witches surrounded me.

3

I went cold.

I jerked from Grace's grasp, taking a large step back and almost tripping on my feet.

"What is this?" My eyes fixed on someone I recognized. "You!"

"I told you I would see you again," Starla said. Her lips peeled back, and I half expected to see fangs for teeth.

On instinct, I called the magic inside my veins. Even if it was weak, I wouldn't go down without a fight.

"Hazel," Grace said, her tone flat.

I stared at her. Oh my God, she brought me here. She had made me trust her so she could sneak me out of the castle and right into dark witches' hands!

I clenched my teeth, inhaled through my nose. Despair would take me nowhere. I had to think this through and find a way out. "So ... since when have you been in bed with the dark witches?"

She tsked. "Light witches, dark witches. Why is

someone who can call on the wind a light witch, and someone who can harness dragon magic a dark witch? It's discrimination. We're all just witches."

What?

"Grace, you're scaring her," Starla said.

I puffed out my chest, even though my insides were shaking. "Scaring? I'm not scared of you."

"Right." Her sick smile widened.

"What do you want with me?" First the Brotherhood. Now the dark witches. What was next?

"We want you to come with us," Grace said. "I promise you no harm will come to you unless you harm us first. We have only your wellbeing in mind."

That was hard to believe. "Why should I go with you?"

"Because we want to show you," Starla said. "We're not evil and we need your help."

"My help?"

Grace nodded. "There's a war on the horizon, but this war can be stopped by you, if you choose to do so."

I frowned. She sounded crazier than Moira. "That doesn't make any sense."

"We can't stay here." Grace offered me her hand. "Come with us and we'll explain everything. I promise."

I took another step back, and I almost bumped into a tall, lean witch. "Like you promised to take me to a better place?"

"I did. I brought you here."

"In the castle! I had no intention of leaving! Not until I could prove I'm innocent."

"You can't prove it," Starla said.

"With you here, I can't." And now that I had run with Grace, and she attacked the Light Order—oh, shit—I bet there was a reward for my head.

"Hazel, the Lightgrove coven is naive," Grace continued. "They only see black and white, but there's so much more. The shades of gray within magic are infinite. You must see them all, and you'll only be able to do so if you come with us."

"Why me?" That was the question of the hour, of the month! Starla and Grace exchanged a glance. I hit a nerve. "You could have chosen Laini, Mei, hell, even Sadie or Moira, but no, you went for the weakest witch in the entire coven. You do realize this makes no sense, right?"

"We can help you with that too," Starla said. "If you come with us, you'll recover your magic, your legacy, and your m—"

"Just come with us, Hazel," Grace said in a rush. "The Light Order is almost here, and if we don't go now, they will catch us."

I retreated another step, making sure I passed the two witches at my back. I held my breath, thinking they would stop me but they didn't. They barely turned to look at me.

"And what if I don't come?"

"We won't force you." Grace waved her hand and a small white paper floated in my direction. I snatched it from the air. A business card. "That's my number. Call me when you're ready to talk." She glanced past me, to the alley's opening. "But if you're not coming with us, then you should run before the Light Order arrives and gets you, and you know that if they do, things will be much worse at the castle now."

Because she had brought me here, it had looked like I had escaped.

I was doomed.

She threw my tote at me, and I grabbed it before it hit the ground, smashing my face. When I looked up, the witches were gone.

"What the ...?"

No time to wonder. I hugged my tote, hitched my duffel bag higher on my shoulder, and ran.

4

I RAN THROUGH THE DARK STREETS OF NEW ORLEANS, LOST and confused. At some point, I stopped in another alley, my hands shaking, my feet hurting, and grabbed my cell phone. I used the GPS to locate myself.

I was near Towland, and I knew for sure there was an open pub two blocks from where I stood. I didn't like being alone this late, but I couldn't stay out like this. I knew the Light Order was after me and I needed to gather my wits.

Tired and dirty and carrying my tote and my duffel bag, I entered the pub. A few customers glanced my way, but most of them didn't seem to care. I found a stool at the end of the bar open and sat on it, dropping my bags by my feet.

"Rough night?" the middle-aged bartender asked me.

"Something like that," I muttered.

"How can I make it better?"

I didn't really want anything, but I also didn't think I

should stay here if I didn't order something. "A glass of the house red wine, please."

He nodded and a minute later dropped a glass half full of deep red liquid. "Let me know if you need anything else."

"Thanks."

He turned his back and I sipped from my glass. It shook against my lips because my hands were still trembling, but I forced myself to not drink it all, even though I wanted to. I needed to be alert.

Beside me, two young women talked animatedly. On their other side was a happy couple. On their side, three older men. A mix of people filled the booths and tables around the place.

I was probably well hidden here for now.

I dropped my head to the counter, closed my eyes, and forced myself to think.

Brotherhood, dark witches, kidnapping? What the hell was going on here?

"Miss, are you all right?"

I lifted my head to face the bartender. Concern etched his face.

I offered him a weak smile. "Yeah, I'm fine. Just … tired." And frustrated, mad, confused, lost, numb, and so many other things.

He stared at me for another fifteen seconds before finally answering someone who was calling him from the other side of the bar.

And I head-desked the bar counter again.

What should I do? What should I do? Maybe I should

let the Light Order take me. It would be a bad spot, but I was innocent. If I gave them time, they would see it. They would find out the truth, wouldn't they?

And what about Grace? Were they hunting for Grace too? Was she fleeing for her life now? God, by now the entire Lightgrove coven thought I was helping Grace and the dark witches, that I was one of them.

No, I couldn't let them take me.

My next thought was to go to Sean, but I discarded that. I was sure the Light Order would go to his place first. If he didn't know where I was, then they couldn't hurt him.

I hoped.

But then what was I going to do?

"Hazel."

I straightened so fast, I almost fell off the stool. A big hand pressed to my back to keep me steady. I twisted in my seat and found Shade in impeccable black slacks and shirt beside me.

"What ... how did you find me?"

"I have my ways," he said, solemn. "The Light Order is searching the area. They will be heading this way soon. You should come with me."

The dark witches had asked me to come with them, now Shade. Next, a nice member of the Brotherhood would show up at the door and offer to take me too.

"I don't trust you."

"I know, but remember that if I wanted to kill you, I wouldn't have helped Sean rescue you. Or I would have done so a long time ago."

Right. He had been following me for several months now. "You're a creeper."

"That's one way of seeing it, but once I explain everything, you'll understand."

My eyes rounded. The last time we talked, Shade had deflected several of my questions. "You mean ... you'll answer and explain all of my questions?"

"I will." He extended his hand to me. "You have my word."

Wary, I slipped my hand into his, and a jolt ran through my arm. Not a painful shock, but a realization, a knowing, a connection, a warm feeling. With all certainty, I knew I could trust Shade. It wasn't a spell or a trick. He wouldn't lie to me, ever, and I knew that as well as I knew myself.

"Okay," I said, barely a whisper.

He picked up my tote and my bag from the floor, dropped a $100 bill on the counter, and stepped back to let me take the lead. We exited the pub.

"The car." He jerked his chin to a black sedan parked at the curb. He opened the passenger door for me, put my things in the backseat, then hopped behind the steering wheel.

As he peeled away from the curb, I frowned. "What happened to your cockiness and charm? You're too serious."

"You're about to know the truth," he said, paying attention to the road. "You'll be mad at me for my behavior."

I shook my head. "That doesn't make sense."

"It will."

SHADE DROVE WEST OF NEW ORLEANS, THEN WENT SOUTH on a small road. My nervousness grew with each mile we crossed.

"We're here," he announced as he turned down a long, narrow road.

It was dark out, but in the distance, I could make out the shape of a house and a few lit windows.

"Where are we?"

"A safe place," he said.

"I thought that if I came with you, you would stop being so cryptic."

"I will, once we are inside the house. Though the entire estate is warded, no one can hear or see us inside."

I gulped. "And you're telling me that to make me feel safe, or because you're a serial killer?"

A corner of his lips curled up. "I've missed your sense of humor."

"What?"

Shade stopped the car in front of the house. Now, close by, I could see it better. A white plantation-style mansion in terrible shape, with thick columns on the front porch. Two of the columns looked like they might fall any at second, the windows had broken glass and hanging shutters, the porch steps were crooked or missing, and the paint was peeling. Overgrown grass surrounded the house, and shrubs and vines had spread over the porch and around the columns.

I hopped out of the car, gawking at the house. Even in

this state, this place had to cost a lot of money. How could a familiar afford this? Or perhaps he couldn't. I shook my head. Oh my God, I felt a headache coming.

I needed sleep and to wake up from this freaking night-mare. When I woke up, I would be back at Towland, madly juggling school and the Lightgrove mentoring and trying to squeeze a date with Sean here and there.

Life was simpler then.

And that had been only a handful of weeks ago.

I sighed.

Shade picked up my bags from the back of the car as the mansion's doors opened and two figures walked.

"Hazel!" Andrea called out, her voice as chipper as ever.

"We were worried about you," Brittany said.

I froze in place, staring at both sisters. "What ...?"

"Oh, right." Andrea reached for me. I almost flinched when she wrapped her hand around my elbow.

Brittany stepped to my other side, the porch creaking under her weight, and placed a gentle hand on my back. "Come inside. We have tea and cookies."

"And explanations," Andrea added.

This could be the most creative trap ever, but I had no desire or strength to fight it. I went inside the house with the sisters, Shade trailing behind us with my things.

I stopped short for the hundredth time today. I gawked at the immense and impeccable foyer. The interior of the house ... it was perfect, clean, intact, and lush.

"What?" I turned in a circle, taking in the place.

Smooth, white stone floors, white walls with mirrors or

intricate metal décor, a layered crystal chandelier hanging from the high, vaulted ceiling. A giant wraparound stair led to the second-floor landing. An archway underneath it opened to a what looked like a living room. To the right were double glass doors, and beyond them what looked like a library. To the left, a dining room with a glass table and high-backed chairs for twelve!

"It's an enchantment," Andrea said. "So, people think this house is abandoned."

"They won't come near it because of all the wards we put around it," Brittany added.

I stared from one to another. "You're witches. Have ... have you always known I'm a witch too?"

The sisters exchanged glances. Why the hell did everyone keep doing that? Were there so many secrets I couldn't know? I was sick and tired of it!

I stepped back. "All right, this has gone on too long. I want explanations. Right now."

"We'll tell you everything." Andrea gestured to the living room. "Come sit with us. We can start while Shade fetches us tea." She looked at him. "Right?"

"Yes," he drawled, sounding annoyed. Shade dropped my bags at the base of the stairs and disappeared through the dining room.

The sisters walked to the living room and I followed.

The back wall had several floor-to-ceiling double doors that seemed to open to a porch. I couldn't be sure since it was dark out.

The sisters padded over the thick white rug and sat in two white armchairs beside a huge, white stone fireplace.

The hearth came to the top of my head! I dragged my feet to the white three-seat sofa across the glass coffee table and the armchairs and took a seat.

Everything was white or silver in this place.

"What do you know about Arianna?" Brittany started.

I rolled my eyes. "All light witches, and dark witches for that matter, know about Arianna, and I'm not here to answer your questions. I'm here to get answers to my questions."

"We'll get there, I promise," Andrea said. "But to get there, we need to clarify some backstory."

"Clarify? What do you mean?"

Andrea sighed. "You know that when Arianna was killed by the Brotherhood, Prince Thales arrived as it was happening and he killed the Brotherhood members. He gathered her ashes and vowed to bring her back somehow."

"He was joined by Arianna's best friends, and council members, Anna and Britta, who wanted to help him," Brittany said.

"They also wanted to keep him from growing crazy during his quest."

"It was an obsession."

"It really was."

"And it did get him killed in the end."

"It did."

"We told him it was a trap."

"We did, but there was only one thing on his mind."

"To bring her back."

Andrea nodded. "We wanted that too."

"We really did."

I stared at them. What were they talking about? How ...? I inhaled sharply. "No," I whispered. "It can't be."

The sisters smiled at me.

"I think you got it," Andrea said.

"But ..." I looked at them and they were only twenty years old. "You would have to be seven hundred years old."

Brittany nodded. "That's right." She pressed a hand to her chest. "Finally, we can introduce ourselves to you properly. I'm Britta."

"And I'm Anna." They waved their hands and a veil of magic peeled off them. Their blond hair gained gray streaks, and faint expression lines appeared around their eyes.

Now they looked to be into their forties, maybe fifties.

I held my breath. "This is impossible."

"We're witches, Hazel," Anna said. "Nothing is impossible. It just depends on how powerful you are."

"And in our case, we're very powerful," Britta said.

"We became immortals when we were forty-four," Anna explained. "Back then, forty-four was elderly and it showed."

Britta chuckled. "Nah, we're still better than most."

I pressed my fingers to my temples; a headache started. This was too much.

Shade entered the room from the left with a silver tray and four cups and saucers filled with a faint yellow tea, and a plate of chocolate chip cookies. He put the tray on the glass coffee table, then sat down on the two-seat sofa to my right.

"When Arianna died, they took me in and spelled me so I could turn into a human at will," Shade said, "and so I was immortal like them."

Anna reached for one of the cups. "We needed more people helping us."

Oh, it was going to be hard getting used to calling them Britta and Anna.

"There weren't a lot of people we could trust." Britta grabbed a cookie.

"There wasn't anyone." Anna sighed. "There aren't many today either."

I frowned. "Wait. Are you telling me ... you're still trying to find Arianna's items and resurrect her?"

Britta swallowed the cookie she had been chewing. "Not really."

"Then what?" I asked, curious.

Anna sipped from her tea. "We knew from the beginning that bringing Arianna back from the dead would be an impossible task."

I frowned. "But ... wasn't that what Prince Thales wanted to do? And you helped him?"

"We tried," Britta confessed. She picked up a cup and offered it to me. Absentmindedly, I took it. Then she got the last one for herself. "We wanted to bring her back, and we went on this quest with Thales, hoping, wishing we could find a way to bring her back."

"But even the most powerful witch with the most powerful items can't perform the impossible," Anna said.

"I thought you said nothing was impossible," I said.

Britta threw me an annoyed look. "That was an exaggeration, clearly."

"When Thales died, we realized that the only way to bring Arianna back was to wait," Anna said.

"Wait?" I took a small sip of my tea. Chamomile. They wanted me calm. Not that the tea would help with that. But then, I realized I was famished and grabbed a cookie.

Britta nodded. "Using Arianna's ashes, we cast another powerful spell."

"For her to be reborn," Anna said, her words slow. Flat.

I frowned. "Okay ... it has been seven hundred years. She must have been reborn, right? Several times if you guys didn't turn her into an immortal too."

"Actually, she was reborn nineteen years ago," Britta said.

The three of them watched me with big eyes, as if waiting—

I inhaled deeply and almost dropped the cup. "No. It's impossible."

Anna smiled at me, but it was a sad one. "It is possible. Hazel, you're Arianna."

5

FOR ABOUT TEN SECONDS, I STARED AT THE THREE OF THEM. And then I burst out laughing.

"Good one," I said, between snorts. "You almost got me there."

Anna, Britta, and Shade didn't say anything. They just looked at me, not judging, not concerned, just ... looking. Almost as if bored.

I laughed and laughed, but they never laughed with me. After a minute or two, the laughter died, and a pit opened in my chest.

"No." I shot to my feet and rounded the sofa. I needed space to breathe, to think, to pace.

"Yes," Anna said simply.

But it couldn't. I was no one. I came from a line of weak witches, and—

I sucked in a sharp breath. "The magic wrapped around my own ..."

"It was us," Britta said. "When we cast the spell for

Arianna's soul to be reborn, we set it so our magic would wrap around the reincarnation so she wouldn't be detected before we found her."

"And so she wouldn't hurt herself," Anna added. "Arianna was powerful. I mean, you are ver—"

I waved my hands at her, unsure I was prepared to hear that again.

Me? Arianna? It didn't make any sense.

I glanced at Shade. "Tell them. You're Arianna's familiar. You would have a special connection to her. You would feel it."

"I feel it," Shade said. "You don't."

"See?" I pointed to Shade. "I don't feel it. I don't feel her magic inside me. I don't have her memories." That wasn't entirely true, was it? Just a few moments ago, I had felt like I could trust Shade, like I had a connection with him. Oh, shit.

"The bond with Shade and the memories will come back once we free your magic," Britta explained.

I stepped closer to them and offered them my hands. "Then do it. Free my magic." Now I was even doubting that was true. What if Almae had made a mistake when she looked into me, my future, and my magic? There wasn't anything holding my magic back, but I was like this. Or maybe it was my fear, my stubbornness, my lack of experience?

Anna put her cup aside and held my hands in hers. "It isn't that simple."

"These spells, to make the three of us immortals, to

have you resurrect, to bind your magic ... these were all powerful spells that required a lot of us," Britta said.

"Not just that, but we needed powerful items set in a specific way in powerful places," Anna continued. "To undo the binding spell, we'll need some items and a powerful place again."

I stepped back again, making her drop my hands. "Of course, it isn't simple."

"Hazel," Britta said, her voice the most serious I had ever heard her speak before. "We have no reason to lie to you, no reason to pretend. You know how beloved Arianna is to the light witches. Why would we joke about this?"

I stared at them for a second. Why would they joke about this? No one in their sane mind would. I plopped down on the sofa, suddenly drained.

"So ... you're saying I'm—" I pressed my lips together. Saying this aloud sounded too crazy. "You're saying I'm Arianna, you're my best friends Anna and Britta, and this is my familiar Shade." I glanced at Shade, and he winked at me. "And that to have my memories and my magic back, we need to do some sort of ritual in a place of magic?"

The sisters nodded at each other.

"Pretty much, yes," Anna said.

My eyes rounded as two recent memories came to mind: when the Brotherhood kidnapped me and Maren asked me repeatedly where Arianna's things were, and when Grace took me to the dark witches and they said that if I went with them, they would explain and I would remember ...

"The Brotherhood and the dark witches ... they also think I'm Arianna."

Britta bit down on another cookie and groaned.

"You are Arianna," Anna said, as serious as Britta. I almost rolled my eyes at them. "The Brotherhood doesn't know you're her, but they know you're connected to her. As for the dark witches ... they know."

"How?"

"The lightning strikes," Britta said. "It was a sign. That was a part of our spell we didn't anticipate. It didn't go as planned. The dark lightning struck when Arianna was waking up, when her powers were starting to reveal themselves."

"And that happened to you, didn't it?" Anna asked.

Shade nodded. "I saw you fighting with Starla during her test night. You tapped in a small fraction of your power."

"Why dark lightning?" I asked.

"Because that was Arianna's affinity," Britta said.

I stilled. "Wait. Arianna had a dark witch's affinity?"

"She did," Anna confirmed. "Even though she came from a line of light witches."

"And she was the one who separated the light and dark witches." I snorted. "What a hypocrite."

"Hey, you're talking about yourself," Shade reminded me.

"I'm still not buying that." I wouldn't buy it until they could prove it to me.

"She had her reasons, and they were good reasons,"

Britta said. "You'll remember everything once we do the ritual, and then you'll understand."

I pressed two fingertips to my temples. "Is there any reason the Brotherhood is after Arianna's things, and the dark witches want Arianna for themselves?"

"The most powerful witch from the fourteenth century is reincarnated," Anna said. "The witch that created an entire new coven that stands today as one of the most powerful covens that ever existed. If you were an evil mastermind, wouldn't you try to get your hands on her and control her before she could turn her magic against you?"

I bit my lower lip. It made sense ... what still didn't make sense was the fact that I was Arianna's reincarnation.

Holy shit, if I stopped to consider ... I had to be dreaming. Shade, Anna, Britta, reincarnation, dark magic, the Brotherhood, the dark witches. What else would they tell me now?

Frowning, I glanced at Shade. "If you're Arianna's familiar ..." I looked at the sisters. "Where are your familiars?" Because they had to have them, right? They were as powerful as Arianna.

Anna and Britta exchanged glances. That was getting on my nerves.

"We killed them," Britta confessed.

I stilled.

"The spell we needed to cast, to make us immortal, to make Shade immortal and shapeshift, and to make sure you were reincarnated required a lot of power," Anna said, her voice low.

"They sacrificed themselves for us," Britta said.

I gawked at them. No, that didn't make sense. "But ... the familiar is an extension of the witch. A—"

"The familiar is an extension of the witch's power," Anna cut me off. "And we needed that power."

I frowned, not liking this. My entire life, I had never allowed myself to consider the possibility of having a familiar, but I always thought that if I ever had one, I wouldn't kill it for anything in the world.

And they had killed theirs for Arianna.

For me.

This sounded so cruel, it could only be a sick joke. I pressed my fingertips to my temples again, suddenly exhausted with so much new information. "Anything else?"

Shade stood. "Actually, there is." He glanced at his phone. Arianna's familiar, a black cat from the 1300s, had a freaking phone! "Hang in there."

He dashed to the foyer, and from where I was sitting, I couldn't see much. But I heard as Shade opened the door and greeted someone.

"Where's she?"

I stood, not believing my ears.

"Through here."

Two seconds later, Sean walked under the archway. His eyes found mine and he erased the distanced between us in five long strides.

"I was so worried." He pulled me to him, one arm firm around my back, the other hand cradling my head. I clutched to him, burying my head in his collarbone.

A sob rose to my throat. I didn't know if it was the

exhaustion from being the middle of the night and not sleeping well the previous night, the hunger, the incredible but serious news, but I wanted to cry, especially in the safe space of Sean's arms.

He kissed the top of my head. "You're scaring me."

I inhaled deeply, swallowing the tears, and pulled back to look at him. "It's just ... I was told a lot."

"Not everything yet, though," Shade reminded me. Right. He was about to tell me something else when Sean arrived.

"Shoot," I said, ready to throw in the towel. Could I climb into a bed, go to sleep, and pretend nothing about this was happening?

He looked at the sisters.

Anna showed me a soft smile. "Hazel ... Sean is Prince Thales's reincarnation."

6

I turned in bed and snuggled closer to Sean. Light filtered through the half-closed curtains, signaling it was morning. I didn't care if it was ten in the morning, or four in the afternoon. Right now, right here, I felt safe, comfortable, and loved.

Nothing could make me get up now.

And then my stomach growled.

Sean chuckled, arms tightening around me.

"Shut up," I said, pressing my face to his neck. I grazed my lips on the side of his throat.

He inhaled sharply. "Hazel," he said with a groan.

I pulled back a little and looked at him. His blue eyes met mine, dark and wanting. Desire for him surged. It did constantly, but right now, I wanted to stare at him. To think.

I was Arianna.

Sean was Thales.

Like me, Sean didn't know anything, couldn't

remember anything, until we performed the ritual that would unbind my magic. Then, we both would remember our past lives.

When Anna said the words last night, that Sean was Thales, Sean frowned and asked, "Who?" He took it all in stride.

"That is cool," he said at the end of the story, sounding really pleased.

I hadn't expected him to buy it.

Not even I believed it all.

Later, after the sisters had told us to rest and Shade showed us to one of the suites on the second floor, I asked Sean how he had gotten here.

"Shade called me," he said. "He told me you had left the castle and were hiding with them here. He gave me the address and I asked a friend for a ride."

"At three in the morning?"

Sean shrugged. "He owed me. But, I told him to stop three miles back. I ran the rest of the way."

He had run three miles in the middle of the night, on a dirt road, with a duffel bag across his shoulders, to get here.

To get to me.

My heart overflowed with love.

It was a shame it was so late and I was so freaking tired. Otherwise, I would have shown him how much I appreciated him.

This morning, I wasn't tired. I felt lazy and I wanted to hide from the world, and hiding right here in this bed with Sean sounded like Heaven.

I pushed up and straddled him, my hands on his naked, chiseled chest. Sean's eyes went wide, but he didn't waste time. His hand found my waist, and when I leaned down to kiss him, he met me halfway.

Next thing I knew, I was underneath him and writhing in pure desire and ecstasy.

Sean's fingertips traced my spine. "We should get up."

"It's comfy here."

"I agree, but I heard your belly growl again."

I groaned, embarrassed. It was true and I was famished, but leaving this bed would mean facing everything else that was waiting for us, and I wasn't ready for that.

"Do we have to?" I sounded like a petulant child.

Sean pressed his lips to my forehead. "Not really."

"Then I think we'll stay like this forever. The rest of the world be damned."

A knock came from the door. "Breakfast will be ready in five minutes," Shade said.

We heard his footsteps retreating and I groaned. Did he really have to spoil this moment?

"Come on." Sean nudged me. "We have work to do." He pressed a kiss to my lips and then jumped out of bed.

I scooted back, with the pillows propped behind my back and watched him for a second, in his full naked glory. Holy shit, he was hot.

And apparently, he was my soul mate from our past lives.

It felt like a fairy tale ... though, didn't all original fairy tales end in tragedy? No, this one wouldn't. We would make it work. We would win.

Determined, I pushed off the bed and got ready while finally taking in the room—last night, as soon as we entered, Sean and I were all over each other and I didn't have time, or the desire, to explore the room.

It was a large rectangle with polished wooden floors, a queen-sized bed and light green bedding, two nightstands, a bench at the end of the bed, an armchair between the wide windows, and a floor mirror with a golden frame. Two doors flanked the mirror, one to the spacious white bathroom with a clawfoot bathtub and separate shower, and the other to the closet where we had left our bags, and I found more of my stuff, which apparently had already been brought from my dorm at Towland earlier.

I put on my black leather leggings, thin hot-pink sweater, and my combat boots, and brushed my hair in front of the mirror. Sean stood behind me and placed a soft kiss on my neck. I swooned. Seriously, I loved how sweet he was to me. Was this how Prince Thales was with Arianna? I could easily see why she fell for him despite all odds.

I looked at his reflection in the mirror—he wore dark jeans, a white T-shirt, and black hoodie. His typical clothes, and part of what first attracted me to him.

I turned to him, stood on tiptoes, wrapped my arms around his neck, and pulled him to me.

Hands clasping my waist, he chuckled. "I think we're already late for breakfast."

"They will survive." I brushed my lips on his.

"Hazel." He groaned and captured my mouth, kissing me hard and deep. He broke the kiss and rested his forehead on mine, breathing as hard as I was. "I love you, and I love making love to you, but we really need to go."

I tightened my arms around his neck. "No, we don't."

He pulled back a little and looked into my eyes. "Don't you want to find out if everything they are saying is true? Don't you want to stop the Brotherhood and the dark witches from coming after you? Then we need to be proactive." He tucked a lose strand of my hair behind my ear. "I won't relax until we deal with all of this. I need you to be safe, and this seems to be the only way."

I sighed. "I know, you're right. It's just ... me? Arianna? It doesn't make sense."

"You're amazing. It makes perfect sense." He placed a kiss on my forehead, then slipped his hand in mine. "Now, let's go."

***

WE FOUND THE SISTERS AND SHADE IN THE SMALLER DINING room adjacent to the kitchen—everything white and silver and so big and expensive-looking, I felt concerned about touching anything.

The long table for eight had a white tablecloth, white plates, white cups, glasses, and silverware, and it had enough food for a banquet: bagels, croissants, muffins, cereal, pancakes, eggs, bacon, at least three distinct kinds of juice, coffee, tea, and water.

Anna gestured for me to sit at the head of the table, on one of the high-backed chairs with arms.

"Hm, no." I sat at the middle of the table, on one of the smaller versions of the chairs.

"But you're our leader," Anna said.

"Our queen," Britta added.

My stomach twisted. "No, I'm not. Not yet at least." Not until they proved it to me. "Until then, I'll sit here, and you all will act as if I'm just a normal witch. Okay?"

The sisters exchanged a glance then they nodded at me.

The first five minutes of breakfast were easy and light. We talked about sleeping in this great mansion, finally resting after so long, and the amazing food before us.

"I made it all," Shade said, with a lopsided grin.

"Liar." Anna rolled her eyes. "We bought it all from a small bakery at the outskirts of New Orleans. They are amazing."

"Not all," Britta said. "We made the eggs, the bacon, and the pancakes."

"Right, we did." Anna bit down on a piece of bacon and moaned. I chuckled. After chewing and swallowing, she fixed her eyes on mine. "We should discuss our plans."

I let out a long breath. "You have to tell me what our plans should be, because I'm still processing all of this."

"First thing, we need to break the binding around your magic," Britta said.

I pushed my plate aside, half of my pancakes unfinished. "That will bring on my memories. And Sean's too."

Anna nodded. "It should."

"Should?" Sean asked.

"We've never done this before," Anna explained. "The theory is simple and should work."

"And if it doesn't?" I asked.

"Then you'll have your powers, but not your memories," Britta said.

I frowned. Could I be Arianna if I didn't remember being Arianna? "And after I have my powers and hopefully my memories back ... then what? I go back to the Light Castle, show them I didn't help the dark witch escape, and continue as normal?"

Anna chuckled. "If you get your memories back, then you'll be a celebrity. Nothing will be back to normal."

"And the Brotherhood and the dark witches' efforts will increase tenfold," Britta added.

"I understand them wanting me while I'm still weak and don't remember anything, but once my magic and my memories are restored, won't I be their biggest enemy? Why would they try to capture me? They would try to kill me instead."

"Besides the prospect of capturing you and forcing you to use your power for their own advantages, we think there's more going on that we don't know about," Anna said.

"What do you mean?" Sean asked.

"They are plotting but we don't know what it is," Britta said. "We've tried finding out, but they are being too quiet about it, and we couldn't risk being made. Besides, right now our focus is unbinding your magic and getting back your memories. The rest can wait for later."

I nodded. "And how do we do that?" They had mentioned a special place and a ritual last night.

"We need a place of power and a witch's wand," Anna said.

My eyebrows shot up. "A wand?" I had heard stories about witches having wands, but I had never seen one. Light witches didn't have wands.

"And not any wand, a queen witch's wand," Britta said.

"Okay," I said. "Where do we find one?"

Anna smiled. "At the Midnight Cauldron."

***

THE MIDNIGHT CAULDRON LOOKED THE SAME—A SMALL shop tucked in the French Quarter crowded with shelves, overstuffed with crystals, cards, threads, beads, books, and potions, most of them fake.

Two women browsed the shelves lined with crystals, each one with a different blessing. One looked at the red endless lover crystal, while the other held the green abundant fortune one. Most of the voodoo shops in the French Quarter were fake, but I knew Khalisa had put real blessings on those crystals, even if little ones.

"My child." Her voice came from the back of the store. There she stood, behind the counter. A smile tugged at her dark lips, and I noticed there were red and orange threads entwined among her dreadlocks. I had not expected to see much of any color on her attire besides black, brown, and white. "I've been waiting for you."

I frowned as I approached her. "Have you been in on this since the beginning?"

Sean, Anna, Britta, and Shade halted behind me.

Khalisa narrowed her dark eyes. "You mean, since the first time you came to see me?" I nodded and she shook her head. "No, my child. I only found out the truth when Anna and Britta came to see me a couple of weeks ago. They told me they would need my help." She glanced at the sisters. "I'm guessing the time is now?"

"It is," Anna said. She stepped beside me, and I startled. I still had this idea that I would suddenly look at her and her sister, and they would be Andrea and Brittany again. But now I knew that had been an illusion for my sake.

"We know you're a Wildthorn witch," Britta said.

Khalisa looked around the shop. The two young women were nowhere to be seen, and apparently, they had taken the crystals with them. Khalisa had once told me all her items were enchanted to do exactly the opposite if stolen. Poor women.

The witch doctor ushered around the counter, past the bead curtain that led to the back room. We spread out around the small room, all of us looking at Khalisa.

"What do you need?" Khalisa asked.

"We need you to tell us where to find your coven," Anna said. "We need the queen witch's help."

"The Wildthorn is a reclusive coven," Khalisa said. "I can call, but they might not receive you."

"We can deal with that," Britta assured her. "Just tell us how to find them and let them know we're coming."

"All right." Khalisa picked up a notepad from one of the tables along the wall, wrote something, and handed the paper to the sisters.

Anna took it. "Thank you, Khalisa. We won't forget your help."

"It is an honor." Khalisa glanced at me. "Especially if that means bringing your full self back."

I frowned. "You think they are right?" I didn't mean to ask that out loud, but the words were out before I could stop them.

"I think that Anna and Britta wouldn't be wrong about this."

7

THE TRIP TO THE WILDTHORN COVEN WAS LONG AND BORING, and almost uncomfortable. Shade took the wheel of the black sedan, and Anna sat beside him in the passenger seat, while Britta, Sean, and I occupied the back seats. Even though the car was large, and the leather seats were comfortable, I felt squeezed between them, and often leaned closer to Sean. Mostly because I wanted to touch him.

Per Khalisa's instructions, we drove northwest toward the middle of the country. "This will guide you," she had said, handing a small green stone to Anna. The rock now was in Shade's shirt pocket, and he said he could feel it tugging, like a rope, directing him where he should drive.

So creepy.

We left the car on what seemed an abandoned ranch along a quiet and broken road, then followed the over-grown trail behind the falling-to-pieces house. Under the afternoon's warm sun, we hiked for over two hours on the winding trail that took us deeper and deeper into the forest, barely talking.

Despite being several hundreds of years old, Anna and Britta were barely winded. That was the beauty of being immortal. Shade had decided to take the track as a cat, and Sean seemed to be taking a stroll through the mall. Damn him and his impeccable body and fitness.

As for me, I cursed every three seconds, either because my shoes weren't appropriate for this and my feet freaking hurt, or because I tripped or twisted my ankle in this terrain.

I refrained from asking "are we there yet?" several times. But only because I didn't want to sound like a child, and because I knew the witches weren't sure. Khalisa's instructions hadn't been specific.

After another twenty minutes, Shade shifted into his human form. "Stop," he said, and we all obeyed him.

Two women jumped from the trees and stared at us. They wore green pants and vests with lines of green paint on their cheeks.

"We're Khalisa's friends," Anna said.

One of them nodded. "We've been expecting you." The duo stepped aside, creating an opening between them. "This way."

Anna, Britta, and Shade didn't hesitate. They marched past the witches. Hand in hand with Sean, I held my breath, half expecting them to throw some magical bolts at us as we passed.

About ten yards later, the trees opened to a valley with lots of trees and houses with brown roofs. On the way,

Anna and Britta had explained that the Wildthorn witches practiced earth magic and were in tune with nature.

"Through here." One of the witches pointed to the stone path carved in the valley. "A witch will be waiting for you at the end of the path."

As we went down the path, the trees and houses grew closer and larger. Vines wound around tree branches; colorful flowers sprouted from every corner. The sides of the houses were covered by ivy and other plants. A canopy of trees surrounded us, and a witch appeared at the end of the path.

"Hello, I'm Neva." Like the others, she was wearing green slacks and a vest, but hers was more intricate. She also wore wrist braces and boots. Her long, dark blond hair was tied in a loose braid with flowers woven through it. "I'll take you to Queen Yira. Follow me."

We followed her through the trees. They became scarcer, revealing the roads and houses between. These were earth witches, and I shouldn't be surprised, but with their dirt roads, stone paths, wooden houses, and overgrown vegetation, I felt like we had gone back in time, to a pre-industrial village.

Everywhere we looked, witches came out of their homes—women, men, and children—all dressed in earth-colored gowns and suits.

Neva guided us down a narrow road that ended in what looked like the largest treehouse in the coven. It wrapped around at least two dozen trees and was three stories tall.

Two witches and two men guarded the main door.

Neva gave them a slight head nod, and they moved aside, letting us pass.

We encountered two guards inside the tree house, but to my surprise, Queen Yira was alone on what looked like a mix of porch and sitting room. A round table for six stood to the left, and to the right wooden armchairs were turned to the impressive view: the valley spread out, revealing a blue lake below. Its surface glowed with the sun shining high, and the green around it was thick and strong.

"Come in," the queen said. "I'm Yira, queen witch of the Wildthorn coven." She glanced at each one of us. "And you're Britta, Anna, the familiar Shade and ..." She smiled when saw Sean and me. "The legendary Queen Arianna and Prince Thales."

"Legendary?" I asked, my voice low.

"You certainly are for founding such a powerful coven, and Prince Thales for supporting a light witch during the witch hunts and for all he has done for her after her death. But most of all, it's your love that is legendary." She glanced at our joined hands. "I see your love survived the centuries."

I glanced at Sean, my cheeks warming. "If we really are Arianna and Thales, I would like to think so."

"Hm." She gestured to the chairs. "Please sit."

The chairs were arranged in a half circle overlooking the incredible view. The queen took the one on the far left, I sat beside her, Sean was next to me, then Shade, Anna, and Britta. Two chairs on the right corner remained empty.

Neva stood at the corner of the room, her posture perfect and her eyes sharp.

The queen continued, "Would you like anything to drink? To eat?"

I looked at the others and they all shook their heads. I frowned. It had been hours since we last ate, and I knew that if we didn't ask, my friends would stay another several hours without anything again.

"Yes, Your Majesty," I said. "We would like some water, please."

She smiled at me, a warm grin that made me feel almost at ease. "I'll ask my maids to prepare a snack for you after our conversation." She looked at Neva, who nodded once. Then the queen crossed her legs and leaned back on her chair. "Now, Khalisa told me you need my help."

"Yes," Anna said. "We bound Arianna's magic for her safety. We need a place of power and a witch's wand to perform the ritual to unlock it."

The queen tilted her head. "There are many places of power in this country."

"Yes, but there aren't many witches with wands," Anna said.

"True." Queen Yira nodded. "I can think of only a couple of covens in which the queens have wands, and most of them wouldn't be willing to help. A few of my witches are powerful enough to have wands of their own, though."

"We need a queen's wand," Britta corrected.

"I see." She considered it. "What would happen if this magic remained bound?"

Anna glanced at me. "Hazel wouldn't have access to her full magic and none of her memories, and the Brotherhood of Purity and the witches of the Darkmist coven would continue to hunt her, thinking she could assist them in whatever evil they have planned. They will torture her, but she will be defenseless against them."

"Hm." The queen looked out at the view. "I'm assuming this ritual is dangerous?"

"It's not dangerous, Your Majesty," Anna said. "It's just lengthy and tedious. We'll need space, quiet, and focus."

She pointed to the mountain in the distance. "Right there, among those emerald green trees ... you can't see it from here, but there's a small clearing there with some enchanted stones and magical flowers. I go there once a week to meditate and recharge. That is a powerful place. You can go there." She stood and stopped in front of me. Then she pulled out a long, crooked stick from a hidden pocket in her skirt. She offered it to me. "And this is my wand."

I gawked at her, at the wand. "Just like that?"

She smiled at me and pulled the wand back. "Almost. I'll go with you and watch the ritual. I'll lend you my wand at the appropriate time, and once it's done, I'll get it back promptly."

"It'll be an honor to have your presence during the ritual," Britta said, sounding excited.

The queen pocketed the wand. "I think the honor will be mine."

RIGHT BEFORE THE SUNSET, AND AFTER A QUICK BUT YUMMY snack, Queen Yira, Neva, along with four women and two men, escorted us to the clearing in the woods. The moment we crossed the last line of trees, I felt it. The peace and power of this place. Besides the feeling, the clearing was small and quaint. Small gray stones formed a wide circle in the center and beautiful pink and orange flowers sprouted between the stones. Tiki torches made of twisted vines were planted along the tree lines. The Wildthorn witches went around the clearing, lighting them. Here, the grass was greener, the air smelled fresher, the breeze blew gentler. I think that even if they hadn't told me, I would have known this place was special.

"This is my private corner," the queen said, walking farther into the clearing. "I don't invite a lot of people here."

"Thank you for making an exception for us," Anna said quickly.

The queen nodded. "I also don't lend my wand to anyone." She fished her wand from her pocket again. "But I confess I want this to work, so ..." She handed it to Britta.

"Thank you, Your Majesty," Britta said, holding the wand as if it was made of crystal.

"You can start when you're ready. My witches and I will stand out of your way." She retreated to one side of the clearing, near the tree line, and her witches flanked her.

I wondered if they were there because they were curious, or to make sure we didn't destroy the place, or run with the wand.

Shade gestured for Sean to go with him. Sean squeezed my hand once, then went with the familiar. They stood along the tree line with Queen Yira and the other witches, but on the other side of the clearing.

"Hazel, sit in the circle," Anna directed.

I let out a long breath. Of course, it had to be inside the circle. When wasn't a witch's circle involved?

I stepped into the circle and sat on the soft grass, my legs folded under me. The sun fell fast now and the light coming from the torches flickered, creating long, moving shadows over the clearing.

I shook my head and focused. This wasn't about funny shadows. It was about the ritual, which should be performed at sunset.

"Ready?" Britta asked.

I nodded and clasped my hands together over my legs. Holy shit, this was happening. If they were right, I would soon have Arianna's magic and memories. That should too crazy, even for me.

A tiny sliver of me still doubted they were right, and now it was time for the truth.

Anna and Britta stood together outside the circle, their hands outstretched in front of them and the wand lying on their palms.

The sisters closed their eyes and chanted, "*Revertere Magicae*," over and over, their voices low. I sat there, watching and waiting. Was I supposed to feel something already?

Suddenly, the sisters opened their eyes. They shone like two flashlights and the wand emitted the same white light from its very tip.

"Hazel—" Anna shut her mouth and snapped her head to the side.

A second later, men dressed in black wearing crimson cloaks emerged into the clearing.

"Protect the queen!" Neva yelled. Instantly, she and the other Wildthorn witches closed in around Queen Yira.

"And we protect ours," Anna whispered as she grabbed my hand and pulled me up. Sean, Shade, and Britta stepped to our side.

The Brotherhood men, over two dozen of them, ran at us with a growl at their lips and their weapons raised.

A sliver of fear ran through me.

But I shouldn't have worried. What was twenty-four human men against thirteen of us?

Neva, Anna, and Britta took charge and stepped forward before the invaders could reach us. Neva called up vines from the ground to wrap around the men's legs and stop them, or at least, slow them down. Anna and Britta shot small glowing darts at the men, incapacitating them.

Then, one of them rose his hand high, a red glowing orb in his palm. The orb blinked three times, and the men pulled masks over their faces. I frowned ... what? The orb exploded, sending thick, red smoke everywhere. The smoke filled my lungs, making me cough, and it burned my eyes.

Confusion reigned for a moment, grunts and screams echoed in the clearing. Sean's hand tightened around mine, and he tugged me back. We scurried a few steps and right into the arms of two men.

"Gotcha," one said as he wrapped a hand around my throat and another on my waist.

"Let her go!" Sean shouted. The other man grabbed for him, but with his martial arts skills, Sean snaked out of his reach, only to strike the man square in his diaphragm, robbing him of air. Sean elbowed the man's back hard and when he fell to the ground, Sean stepped between his shoulders, a loud crack noise resounding from it.

I gathered my magic and was about to shock the man holding me, when he retrieved a knife out of the nowhere and pressed the blade to my neck. "Try anything funny and you'll die right here."

"You want me alive," I croaked, afraid of moving too much and being cut.

"But no one said anything about not hurting you." He pressed the knife a little more.

Moving as little as I could, I reached up and rested my hand on his. I sent a jolt of lightning into him. The man yelped and his hold slackened enough for me to slip away, but not before he slashed away with the knife and scratched my shoulder. I gasped as the pain ricocheted through my arm. Like a viper, Sean shot out from behind me and punched the man in the nose. His eyes rolled and blood sipped from his nostrils. The knife fell to the ground, a second before the man did.

"Are you okay?" Sean asked, grabbing my arms.

I flinched. "I think so."

Sean pursed his lips, his eyes on the thin red line on my shoulder. "It doesn't look deep."

"I'll be fine." I glanced up at him. He had a split lip, even though I hadn't seen anyone striking against him. "How about you?"

"I—"

A grunt came from our side, and Shade emerged from the smoke, pouncing on the back of a Brotherhood member like a cat.

"Another one down," he said, rather proud.

The smoke dissipated slowly, and we started seeing the confusion around us. Shade was pristine, as if he hadn't just fought for his life. Britta looked okay, though Anna leaned against her, a splash of deep red on her side.

I gasped and went to her. "On no."

"It's okay," Anna said through gritted teeth. "I'm immortal, remember? I can feel it healing already. Give it ten minutes and it'll be closed."

The smoke retreated.

The Wildthorn witches were mostly fine. The queen looked okay, Neva had some bruises, and only two of them had wounds. Queen Yira sent them away to get treated. Most of the brotherhood members were dead at the Wildthorn witches' feet.

"How did they find us?" I asked, my stomach flipping at the sight of so much blood and carnage.

"I don't know," Britta whispered.

"The point is, they found you," Neva said. "Whatever you're here to do, do it quickly." She walked toward us, and with the help of the two males in their group, picked up two of the Brotherhood members we had knocked out.

Queen Yira took a few steps to the side. She crouched down, picking up her wand from the ground. She held it out, two pieces, one on each hand. "My wand is broken."

8

A HEAVY BALL SETTLED IN MY STOMACH. "NO," I WHISPERED. I took a step toward the queen. "I'm so sorry. This is my fault."

The queen turned hard eyes at me. "It was, but I'm a woman of my word. Now that the threat is gone, you can continue with the ritual, finish it, then be gone."

"But the wand," Anna muttered.

"I'm an extension of the wand, and the wand is an extension of me," the queen said. "I'll hold it and you hold on to me. Use my magic to finish this. It might not work perfectly, but it should work."

"Your Majesty, about—"

She glared at me and I shut up. "Just get this over with."

We all moved into the same positions we were before the attack, except for the queen now stood between Anna and Britta, holding the two broken wand pieces. Anna and Britta rested their hands on the queen's and glanced at me.

"Are you ready?" Britta asked.

I hesitated for a moment. What if there were more brotherhood members hiding in the forest? One of the Wildthorn witches had gone to check, but she could have been attacked, or she might not find them in time. Besides, now with the broken wand, would this really work?

I wouldn't argue with them, though.

I sat in the middle of the circle and waited.

The sisters began chanting. This time, Queen Yira joined them. "*Revertere Magicae*," they said, low and fast.

They opened their eyes, shining like the wand's broken tips.

I held my breath, expecting something to go wrong but it didn't. Their chanting grew louder, their words faster, and the light shone brighter.

Suddenly, the gray stones on the ground shone a bright white light, and even flowers shifted into shades of neon. White lines slithered through the grass, from the stones directly to me.

I held my breath, a little wary, but when the lines reached me, they didn't hurt. All I felt was immense power entering me. I closed my eyes and focused on it. My instinct was to fight it, but I held on and let it do its job. It traveled within me, searching for something, for my magic and the binding around it.

The power reached my chest and I gasped. It found the binding, cutting it. The chanting grew louder, the power increased, its force making me gasp. I leaned forward, a hand on the ground for support.

"Hazel!" Sean shouted.

"Stay put," Shade said. "She'll be fine."

I wasn't so sure about that.

The foreign power searched for an opening. It prodded, it poked, and then it attacked the binding again. My chest hurt like it was being ripped open from the inside. I screamed and fell back on the grass, writhing in pain.

Sean and Shade argued, but I couldn't make out their words, my mind lost to the pain.

The scissors cut and cut and cut, as if it were a dull knife sawing a thick rope. Just a little more ...

The binding snapped, the pain and the power left, and I inhaled deeply.

I stayed on the ground afraid of moving and bringing the pain back.

"Hazel?" a voice called.

I peeked through my lashes and found Sean, Shade, Anna, and Britta hovering over me.

"Are you okay?" Anna asked.

"I ... I think so," I said.

Sean crouched beside me, hooked an arm around my waist, and helped me up. "Are you sure?"

I nodded. Then I stilled for a moment, feeling inside of me. The binding was gone, but it hadn't been an explosion of power like I had thought it would be. It was more like a hole in a giant sandbag and a few sand grains dripped from it.

I frowned. "Did it work? Because I don't feel the magic, and I don't—"

Sean's hand slipped into mine and an image flooded my mind.

My blonde tresses blew in the wind as I stood at the top of a hill under the bright moonlight. I braced myself, my gown thin for the chilly night, and looked up at the stars. The crunching of leaves startled me, and I turned to the sound, only to see Prince Thales walking toward me.

"Sorry," he said, his voice rough but gentle. "I didn't mean to startle you."

I smiled. "I knew it was you."

Thales didn't stop when he reached me. He stepped right into me, hooked his arm around my waist, and pulled me to him. "I see you're cold. I can warm you up."

I blinked and the memory faded.

"Did you see that?" I asked, breathless.

Sean nodded. "I did."

My eyes filled with tears. There were no other memories so far, but I was sure of two things: I was Arianna, and I loved Sean and had loved his soul for centuries.

Sean wrapped his arms around me. "I don't know what to make of that, but damn, it feels good to be here with you."

"Ditto." I buried my head in his neck. "You look the same. I hadn't noticed before how you look like the pictures and painting we see of Princes Thales in books and such, but now I see it. You're exactly the same."

"And so are you," he said, his arms still tight around me. "You're still the same stunningly beautiful woman."

Someone cleared their throat. Sean and I pulled back a little but held hands. We were together again, and it felt divine.

"See? You are Arianna," Anna said, her voice catching.

Britta's eyes brimmed with tears. "We told you so."

"I guess I am." Wow, that was weird. I couldn't believe I was THE Arianna! I frowned. "But I don't feel powerful, and I had only one memory."

"If I may," Queen Yira said. "That was the effect of having the wand broken. If it had been whole, the ritual would have worked perfectly."

Britta nodded. "The binding is gone. Now it's only a matter of time. Your powers and your memory will come back, albeit slowly."

I hoped they were right. It was odd to know I had so much more in me, that I was so much more, but I couldn't access it.

I looked at the queen. "I'm so sorry, Your Majesty." I really meant it. "If there's anything we can do for you, please let us know. And I promise you, once I have access to my magic and memories, if you still haven't mended the wand, I'll come back and help you find a way to do it."

She sighed. "Let's hope I can fix it on my own." She glanced at each one of us, not hiding how annoyed she was. "Now that you have what you came here for, you're welcome to leave."

"Of course, Your Majesty," Britta said. She gestured for us to follow her.

"Thank you, Queen Yira," I said before following the others.

She didn't say anything. I understood why. After we came here and she welcomed us as guests, her wand had been broken. If it were me, I probably wouldn't have helped us after that.

But I was glad she did.

Britta and Anna fashioned magical flashlights out of sticks they found on the ground, and we hiked the forest in the dark and in silence. Well, as silent as a forest could be, especially with us walking, crunching dried leaves, and tripping over tree roots.

It was past midnight when we finally piled into the sedan, and Shade started driving back to Louisiana.

"Aren't you too tired to drive?" I asked him. "We could stop at an inn, rest for the night, and continue tomorrow morning."

"I'm fine," was all he said.

Everyone was probably tired, but after a few minutes, when I looked around the car, no one was sleeping.

"What now?"

Anna looked at me. "Now we go back to our place and try to jolt your memory and spark your magic."

"How?"

"Probably training and a walk down memory lane," Britta answered.

"We have a lot of work ahead of us," Anna said. Britta nodded.

With a sigh, I rested my head on Sean's shoulder.

That sounded exhausting. But if it meant, I would get my powers and my memory back, so be it. I would face whatever was coming our way.

9

―――――

THE ONLY TIME SHADE STOPPED THE CAR WAS EARLY IN THE morning, when everyone needed to use the bathroom and breakfast. We had a thirty-minute break at a rest stop, then continued the drive.

Sean asked him if he wanted to switch, and I asked him again if he wanted to stop at an inn so we all could get a proper rest, and again his answer was no.

Finally, a little past noon, we arrived at the mansion, and even though most of us had slept for the duration of the drive, we all went directly to bed.

Well, not directly ...

I was in desperate need for a shower and asked Sean if he wanted to join me.

"You don't have to ask twice."

As we advanced toward the bathroom, our clothes met the floor. I entered the shower first and turned the water on, but Sean didn't let me get wet. He rammed into me, pushing me against the tiled wall.

The moment his mouth met mine, I was transported somewhere else.

Naked against a smooth rock in the middle of a lake, I looked up into Thales's eyes, the desire clear in them despite the cover of the night. He leaned into me, his body pressing against mine. I barely noticed the waterfall behind him, or how warm the water was against our skin, not when he was touching me like that, every inch of him covering me.

His lips found mine but only for a quick moment. "I love you," he whispered in my ear, then glided his lips to my throat, and his hand down to my legs.

I moaned.

"I love you," Sean whispered. "More now than back then."

I blinked and stilled. "Did you see that?"

Sean nodded. "I did. And I'll repeat. When I'm in Thales's skin, I can feel the immense love I felt for you. The crazy desire. The intense sense to protect you." He cupped my face. "But it's all tenfold now."

My chest tightened and tears brimmed in my eyes. "I love you too."

"Now ..." He dragged his lips across my neck. "Where were we?"

I gasped as his hand mirrored the memory and found my core. I held on to him with all I had and let him do whatever he wanted with me. When we finally made it under the water, it was warm on our skin, but our bodies entwined and moving together as one was a lot hotter.

A RINGING WOKE ME UP.

Dazed, I turned in Sean's arms and found my phone on the nightstand. The room was dark, and I glanced at the time as I picked up my phone—it was seven in the evening.

Shit, we had slept too long.

An unknown number showed as the caller ID. I frowned and answered, "Hello?"

"It's me." Grace's voice came through the speakers. I sat up, suddenly alert.

I shouldn't be surprised she had my phone number. I bet she had studied my entire file at the Light Castle.

"What do you want?"

"To ask you if you reconsidered."

I snorted. "To join you?"

"If not to join me and my sisters, then to hear us out."

"And walk into a trap?"

"I wouldn't stoop so low."

I doubted that. "How is the hiding life?"

"Who says I'm hiding?"

I blinked. "You attacked the Light Order warriors. They—"

"No one saw me," she said, sounding rather proud. "They only saw you. They are hunting you. As for me, I'm still at the castle, as I have always been."

I gasped. "What the ...? I'll tell them, then. I'll call them right now and let them know it was you!"

Sean stirred beside me.

"Do you think they'll believe you? First, you visited Starla without permission, then you freed ghosts, again without permission. Starla asked for you right before she escaped, and the Light Order saw you attacking them before fleeing the castle."

Shit, she was right. If she had cast some sort of spell to hide or disguise herself while she was taking me out of the castle, then I looked like the guilty one.

And she remained inside the Light Castle, working against the light witches.

"I'll find a way to expose you."

She chuckled. "Good luck with that." She paused. "Last chance, Hazel."

"Never," I snapped.

"You've been warned." She ended the call.

I stared at my phone.

Sean reached for me, smoothed his hand down my back. "Hey, what happened?"

"It was Grace," I said.

He sat up, now as awake as I was, and I told him what she had told me.

"Shit," he muttered.

"My thoughts exactly." I pushed away from the bed and found some clean clothes. "Come on. Let's grab something to eat and see if the others are awake. They need to know about this call."

I SHOULDN'T BE SURPRISED TO FIND ANNA, BRITTA, AND Shade at the kitchen, putting together dinner—a fancy takeout they had gotten from a restaurant. I sort of imagined they would all be sleeping, especially Shade.

"Good evening, sleepyhead," Anna said with a smile.

"Dinner is almost ready," Britta said. She had her back to us and was fussing with the takeout boxes. "You can go sit down and we'll bring it over."

"How can we help?" Sean asked.

"Table is set," Shade said. "And we're bringing the food in a minute." He shooed us with his hands.

Sean and I reluctantly walked to the table adjacent to the kitchen and sat in the same places from yesterday morning.

The sisters and Shade brought a huge pan with spaghetti and meatballs and garlic bread and shredded cheese to the table along with red wine, then they took their seats.

"Dig in," Anna said.

Trying to be considerate, I waited for about five minutes—when everyone had already served themselves and some of us were already halfway through our portions —before I said anything.

"I got a call from Grace this evening," I started.

Anna, Britta, and Shade froze mid chewing or drinking. After swallowing, Shade cursed, Anna bristled, and Britta took a deep breath.

"And?" Britta asked, reaching for more wine.

I told them what she said about wanting to talk, and about how she was still at the Light Castle because no one had seen her that night. No one knew she was a dark witch working against the Lightgrove coven.

"We need to warn them," I said, then explained what Grace told me about my street credit. If I tried to warn them, they wouldn't believe me. Hell, I wouldn't believe me.

"We can find a way to send them a letter or some other warning sign," Anna said. She drank a sip of her wine. "I can make it look like something they can't ignore."

"How?" I asked.

Anna shrugged. "We'll think of something."

Britta narrowed her eyes at me. "She wants to meet. Do you want to meet with her?"

I shook my head. "No way in hell. She's tricked me. Besides, she's a dark witch."

"Remember, you have a dark witch's affinity," Anna said.

I frowned. "But I was born from light witches, wasn't I? In this life and in the previous one?"

Britta nodded. "As far as we know, yes."

"Then that's not my fault," I said. "Besides, I chose the light witches' side. That should count for something."

"Once you recover all of your memories, you'll understand," Anna said.

"Speaking of which, have you remembered anything else?" Britta asked.

I glanced at Sean and my cheeks warmed up. "Other than a few moments between Prince Thales and Arianna, no."

She nodded. "Don't worry. It'll all come back."

"All right, and what do I do in the meantime?" I asked, getting irritated. This entire thing was still crazy and had uprooted my life. At first, the goal was to recover my magic and my memories and go from there, but that hadn't happened. "Sit here and wait? What if it takes months, years for my memories to come back?"

"That's why we should try to jog your memory," Anna said. "So, it happens sooner rather than later."

"What happens sooner rather than later?" Sean asked. He usually didn't butt in much on the witches' conversations, but now he knew he was Prince Thales. He had been a part of all of this since the beginning.

The sisters shrugged.

"We don't know for sure," Anna said. "Whatever the Brotherhood and the dark witches are planning, it must be big, but we don't know what it is. We just know they will do anything to get their hands on you."

I didn't like this. "So, I'm supposed to be a prisoner in this house until I master my powers and recover my memories?"

"You're not a prisoner," Britta said. "You're the first goddamn queen of the Lightgrove coven, and I'm sure that when your powers are restored, you'll be more powerful than Queen Denise."

Anna snorted. "Probably twice, if not three times more powerful than Denise."

I stilled, my eyes wide. That much power? That much magic? It seemed unimaginable. Impossible.

"But now that we know who I am, can't we at least warn the Lightgrove witches about Grace?" I asked. "There must be a way to convince them of the truth."

"I said I will send them a warning," Anna said.

"But you don't know if it'll get in the right hands. What if Grace intercepts it? Now thinking about it, she's probably not the only one undercover in the castle." I gasped. "Oh my God, Moira tried to get me out of the castle before Grace did. She's one of them! When she couldn't, Grace stepped in. And if Moira is, then I'm sure there are more. We need to warn them."

"This isn't good," Anna observed. "If there are dark witches in the castle, then it would be easy for them to attack from within and take over."

"All right, we hear you," Britta said. "We'll reach out to Queen Denise first thing in the morning and demand an audience, even if we have to lie about a major threat."

"If you talk about the real threat, then it's no lie," I said.

Britta nodded. "Right. We'll do that."

I frowned. "Couldn't we tell them the truth? That I am Arianna?" My voice caught at the name. I wasn't used to it. "Grace already knows, and all the dark witches working on the inside. If we told Queen Denise and the others, then they might drop the charges against me and do something. They can help us fight the dark witches and the Brotherhood."

"We thought of that," Anna said. "But we're afraid we don't know who to trust. What if the queen and the entire council are in on it? We can't risk it."

"Until we can do more on our own, we need to be careful," Britta added.

I hated this. I hated how powerless and useless I felt.

We finished eating in silence, though no one seemed interested in food anymore. After dinner, Shade, Britta, and Anna said they would clean up and told us to relax on the back porch, where a fire pit was lit around several wicker chairs with high backs.

Sean and I exited to the porch and a chill breeze whipped around us. It was late fall and despite the warm days, the nights were getting colder. Great to sit down on a chair with Sean and snuggle in front of the fire.

Sean wrapped his arm around my shoulder and pulled me to him, so my side was entirely glued to his. I rested my head on his shoulder.

Then the image in front of me changed.

I was seated at the top of a hill, a hill I had climbed so many times before. The moon shone high in the sky, and despite all the unease brewing inside of me, I was content right now. Mostly because Thales was seated by my side, his arm secured around my waist and my head on his shoulder.

It was perfection.

I blinked and came back to the present.

"Did you see that?" I asked.

Sean nodded. "I did. I guess we'll start seeing more of those now."

I didn't mind that idea. I welcomed it. I was eager to remember more of Sean and the coven and do whatever it was that I was supposed to do.

"I confess I'm a little nervous," I whispered.

Sean turned his face to me. "Why?"

I shrugged. "This whole 'let's kidnap Arianna' thing. I hate it."

He kissed the top of my head. "Don't worry, my love. I won't let anyone kidnap or hurt you."

Even though I was all for girl power and female independence, I did like the idea of having him in my corner and helping me out. Supporting me. Loving me.

I placed my chin on his shoulder. "Ditto."

A quick half grin flashed in Sean's smile before he pressed his lips to mine.

Yup, this was paradise.

10

DESPITE HAVING SLEPT FOR HOURS YESTERDAY, WHEN SEAN and I went to bed after midnight—and made love again— we slept like rocks. Sleeping in his arms night after night had been the best part of it all.

No, scratch that. The best part had been finding out we loved each other in our previous lives and we had found each other and loved each other in this one too.

This time, we woke up early, and after breakfast, Sean decided to go to New Orleans to pick up more of his stuff, maybe some of mine too.

I stood at the front porch, now looking whole and pris- tine when coming from inside the mansion, and Sean stopped at a lower step. Like this, I was almost his height.

"I'll be back in a couple of hours tops." He embraced me.

For some reason, I was apprehensive. If it was up to me, he wouldn't go anywhere, at least not away from me, until we dealt with the Brotherhood and the dark witches.

I grasped the sides of his hoodie. "Be careful."

The sisters had said that leaving wasn't a good idea, but Sean should be okay. Shade said he would go with Sean. We were stronger in numbers.

Shade lowered the window from the sedan. "Are we going or what?"

I spied at him around Sean's shoulder, my eyes narrowed. Instantly, Shade looked ahead, as if he hadn't said anything. I thought that maybe because he was Arianna's familiar—my familiar—he was afraid of me. But that didn't sound right, did it? Familiars and their witches had a special bond, almost like family and sometimes even deeper.

Sean kissed the top of my head. "See you soon." He pressed a soft kiss on my lips before turning and going to the car.

Once the car started moving, he waved at me.

I stayed on the porch until the car disappeared at the bend in the road.

A few minutes later, Anna and Britta appeared beside me.

Anna put a hand on my arm. "Shade will take care of him."

"Besides, Prince Thales could always take care of himself," Britta said. "I bet it isn't any different in this life."

I remembered when Sean had fought the Brotherhood during my rescue and a couple of days ago at the Wildthorn coven and smiled. "It isn't."

"Good," Anna said. "Then we shouldn't waste time."

She poked my forehead. "Let's see if we can jog some of those memories from that pretty head."

I frowned, trying to reconciliate these two were Andrea and Brittany, the good friends I had made in college. If I squinted, I could even see it.

One corner of my lips curled up. "Is that how you treat your queen?"

Her eyes widened and her mouth hung open in a big, amused smile. "What? Was that a joke?"

Britta laughed. "I think it was." She hooked her arm in mine. "Now, let's go."

THE MANSION'S BASEMENT WAS A HUGE UNFINISHED AREA, but since the sisters insisted we shouldn't train outside for safety, the basement it was.

I stood in the center, waiting for a miracle to happen.

"All right," Anna said. She and Britta walked around me, like generals addressing their soldiers. "You now know your affinity is the dark lightning, so it should be easier to reach for it, to find it, to bring it forth."

"Relax and close your eyes," Britta said. I closed my eyes and inhaled deeply. "Now think of yourself like a big claw digging through your chest. There's a box in there, a closed box, but not locked. You're going to open it and release whatever is inside."

Her imagery was pretty good, and I could feel it exactly as she said, but not as fast. It took me a while to find my way to the box, to open it, even if it wasn't locked. But once it was open, a jolt of energy rushed through me.

"Whoa," I whispered, my eyes still closed.

I spied inside the box and saw the dark lightning striking every two seconds, and racing from side to side. It seemed tight in that box, squeezed and hurting. It wanted out.

I reached for it.

I opened my eyes just as my fingertips crackled. I turned my hand, palm up and a small dark lightning struck across my skin. I gasped a chuckle. "Holy shit."

"Nice." Anna smiled at me. "Now, make it bigger."

I focused on the small lightnings cutting over my palm and willed it bigger. The lightning grew an inch, three, five, ten! It grew stronger, more energetic, and unruly. I gritted my teeth, trying to regain control over it.

The dark lightning shot from my palm, hit the ceiling, then flew to the wall, leaving two sizzling holes behind.

I stood still, my eyes wide. "I could have hurt you."

"We are immortal, remember?" Britta said. "It would hurt, but we would be fine."

"Even so, I don't want to hurt you."

"That's what you're focusing on?" Anna asked. "You should be celebrating. Finally, you got hold of your affinity!"

"But I can't control it."

"You didn't expect it would be easy, did you?" Britta asked. She turned to Anna with a big smile. "Remember the first time Arianna got her gift?"

Anna chuckled. "Oh, yeah." She looked at me. "Arianna was ten, one of the youngest in our community to receive her gift. We were in school, which at that time was a spacious room in the middle of the village where the kids studied. There were what ... forty kids?"

"I think fifty," Britta said.

"Right. But only like six of us were witches, and that was a secret, like it is now."

"But there was that bully ..."

I blinked and I was transported to another time.

A big boy with a round belly pushed Anna, her blond hair tied in two braids, against the wall of the building where school was held.

"What did you say, little freak?" he growled at her face.

Britta and I stood to the side, too afraid to act, but we were more afraid of abandoning Anna. Another girl with dark hair had been with us just a second ago, but she ran away.

"Let her go," Britta said, her voice breaking. I knew she was truly afraid of the boy.

Last week, he had punched another girl because he thought she was a witch. Her family got in trouble for it, and they had to prove to the town council that none of the women were witches, but for a moment there, I thought they would be burned at the stake.

She really wasn't a witch.

But Anna was. She had not received her gift yet, but she was.

He pushed her against the wall again, making her cry in pain and fear.

Rage filled my veins. "Let her go!" I yelled.

The boy turned his vicious eyes toward me. Britta and I

were ten, Anna was twelve, but this boy was fourteen. He was a lot bigger and stronger than we were, but at this moment, I wasn't thinking about that. All I wanted was to make him stop, to make him pay.

He let go of Anna and faced me. "Did you talk to me, freak?"

"I did," I said, puffing out my chest. "And I'm not a freak."

"I know you are and I'm going to tell everyone about it." He reached for me, swiped at my hair, and yanked my head forward.

The rage grew inside me, a torrent I couldn't control.

My finger crackled and dark lighting shot from my palms, right at the boy's feet. With a yelp, he let go of me and jumped back. I threw another four lightning bolts at him as he ran away from us.

Anna, Britta, and I looked at each other, huge smiles on our faces.

"You scared him!" Anna said, sounding happy.

Britta looked at me in wonder. "Arianna! You got your gift!"

"I did!" A sudden elation filled my chest, and then it was gone the next second, replaced by pure panic. "Oh shit, now he's going to tell everyone."

I blinked and found myself back in the basement, with Anna and Britta looking at me.

"What happened?" Anna asked.

Britta's eyes widened. "You had a memory."

I nodded. "I did. It was the first time I got my gift, when that bully hurt you." And because of that, my mother moved to another town in the middle of the night. If it had been so horrible for that other family to prove they weren't witches, how terrible would it be for us? Especially because we would have to lie about it.

Thankfully, not one year later, Anna's and Britta's family moved too, and we were reunited.

"That's amazing," Anna said.

"Perhaps we can tell you more stories from our past together," Britta suggested. "Those should spark some memories."

"I would like that, but first ..." I took several steps back and called my magic. Now that I had a memory of myself using it so naturally, the magic answered fast and strong.

My arms crackled with lightning before I threw my hand out and a thick lightning bolt hit the opposite wall. It exploded with a loud boom, cracking the unfinished wall and charring the wood around it. The mansion shook over our heads.

"You did it!" Anna said, excited.

"That is great, but maybe we should move training to the backyard even if it's dangerous," Britta suggested.

I agreed.

WITH A THIN LAYER OF SWEAT ON MY NECK, SHOULDERS, AND in between my breasts, I dragged my feet to the back porch. I had ditched my sweater for a tank top long ago, and at first, the cool October air did wonders.

I reached for the glass of water and my phone on the small wicker table between the rocking chairs. I drank

water and checked my phone. I almost choked when I realized what time it was.

"Sean and Shade have been gone for three hours," I
said. I dropped the glass of water on the table and checked
my phone for messages or calls, but there was nothing.

Anna and Britta walked over to me as they too checked
their phones.

I texted Sean:

> Hey, you. What's taking so long?

I watched the screen, waiting to see the three dots on
the bottom show up. They didn't. So, I called him. The
phone rang several times, then went to voicemail.

"Okay, something is wrong," I said, apprehension
lacing my heart.

Anna lowered her phone from her ear. "Shade isn't
picking up either."

My stomach dropped. "What does this mean?"

The sisters shook their heads. "We can't assume the
worst yet," Britta said.

"Maybe they are driving in a place with bad reception,"
Anna said, her voice unsure.

I raised an eyebrow. "We live in a world full of magic
and evil. Do you really think it would be that simple?"

She didn't answer, but her gaze grew worried.

I opened my mouth to ask what we should do when my
phone dinged.

I opened the messages app and saw a new message
from Grace. I clicked on her name and my heart stopped.

There was a picture of Sean, tied to a chair, his head low, and Shade as a cat at his feet inside a small metal crate.

A text appeared underneath the picture: *Meet us at Hyatt Elementary School at 10 p.m. or we'll kill them both.*

11

I pocketed my phone and marched inside the house.

"Hazel," Anna called me.

"Wait," Britta said. Both women followed me into the living room. "We know what you're thinking."

"You're going to do something stupid."

"Hear us out before you do anything, please."

It was the please that made me stop. Under the archway, I turned to them. "You know I can't sit here and just wait. In fact ..." I picked up my phone. "I'll text Grace and tell her I'll meet her." I glanced over my shoulder at the front door. Shit, Shade and Sean had taken the sedan. "Tell me you have another car somewhere on this property." I opened the maps app to check how long it would take me to walk back to New Orleans. "Otherwise, I'm walking."

"Hazel, listen to yourself," Britta said. "You have to remain—"

"Don't say calm!" I snapped. "I don't want to be calm, not right now. They have Sean! Prince Thales. The love of my life! Do you really think I'll stop and think? I don't want to. I want to go to them right now, zap them all with my lightning, and burn them to the ground."

"Hazel," Anna whispered. "Don't be so rash."

"We understand your frustration, believe me," Britta said. "But we need to come up with a solid plan before we do."

I stared at them. I didn't want a plan, I wanted war. If it depended on me, I would march in there, wherever they wanted me to go, guns blazing, lightning striking, and I would take them all down.

But I had rediscovered my affinity. Several times during the last hour of training, I had lost control and almost struck Anna and Britta. And there were a lot of charred trees behind the house.

Going in there like that would mean my death, and I couldn't help Sean if I was dead.

My shoulders sagged and I dragged my feet back to the couch. I plopped down, suddenly drained of energy. "What is the plan, then?"

The sisters exchanged a glance. I hated when they did that.

"First of all, we don't give in to their demands," Anna said.

I sat up straighter. "What? How—?"

"They won't harm Sean or Shade," Britta said, cutting me off. "They know they need the guys alive if they want you to cooperate."

"So, we don't go at the agreed time," Anna said. I had to suppress a groan. Why were they doing this to me? "We go to the meeting place after they are gone, and trace them to their hideout."

Britta nodded. "Once we know where they are hiding and the place's layout, we'll be able to come up with a plan to get Sean and Shade from there."

"You're talking about ..." I did the math in my mind. "That's way too long." It was a freaking Wednesday. By then, the dark witches could have a tantrum and throw caution aside. "If you're going to come up with a plan, do it now. We need to act as soon as possible."

"We agree on that, but Hazel ..." Anna sat down on the coffee table in front of me and held my hand in hers. "We lost you once already and it took far too long to find you again. We can't risk losing you again. Not yet."

I frowned. "I'm not that important. There are other covens with queens out there. Besides, everyone dies. One day, I will die, even if it's in a hundred and fifty years." Powerful witches were known to live way past a hundred. A few rare ones were known to have made it to two hundred.

Britta shook her head. "No, Hazel. It must be you."

"What do you mean?" Again, the sisters looked at each other. I pointed my fingers at them. "Stop that and just talk to me!"

"We don't know," Anna said, her voice with a hint of sadness. "In the last couple of months before her death, Arianna was hiding something from us."

"It was the first time she ever hid anything from us," Britta added. "We asked her to open up to us several times, but she said there was nothing. She wasn't hiding anything."

"But she was," Anna continued. "We don't know exactly what, but we do know it led the Brotherhood of Purity to our village to find her. She was killed for it."

I gulped. "I ... I don't remember anything."

"The dark witches, the Brotherhood ... they don't know that," Anna said. "They think you're Arianna or someone connected to her, and they want you for that."

"So ... that's why you brought me back?" I shouldn't feel bad about this. I didn't remember them. Well, not much, not yet. "Not because you were my friends."

They stared at me as if I were crazy. "Hazel, no," Britta said. "First and foremost, you were our friend, like a sister to us. We would have done anything for you. And the fact that you're our queen only made everything bigger, more important. Maybe even our feelings, but you can be sure that we wouldn't be this loyal, this deeply entwined with our history, if it weren't because of the relationship we had before you became queen."

It was hard for me to imagine all of that, as I had almost no memories of it. Maybe after a few days, a couple of weeks, I would have remembered enough. But we didn't have that much time.

"Let's put that aside and talk about it again after we rescue Sean and Shade," I said, focusing on what I could. "So, the plan is to skip the meeting, but go there in the middle of the night?"

Anna nodded. "The meet up will probably be near their hideout. It'll be easy to devise a rescue plan, then."

I didn't like it, but I didn't have much choice.

"Okay," I muttered. I turned to the kitchen. "I'll make myself a sandwich and go to bed early. The training and the stress from this situation have taken its toll on me."

"Of course," Britta said. "We'll wake you up half an hour before we leave, so you can get ready."

I glanced their way before opening the pantry's door. "Thanks."

I MADE A SANDWICH, ATE IT BECAUSE I WOULD NEED MY strength, then I went to my bedroom, changing into tight-fitting black clothes, tied my hair into a ponytail, and waited.

If Anna and Britta came to my bedroom to check on me, they wouldn't see any lights from under the door and they wouldn't hear anything. I hoped they thought I was sleeping, not that I was sneaking out.

Because I was sneaking out.

Around nine, I sent a text to Grace:

> I'll come at midnight. Tell me where.

A few minutes later, she texted me the address. I googled it and found it to be a parking lot of an old elementary school that hadn't been in use for many years.

I didn't think the sisters were going to bed tonight, not with a plan to wake up in a handful of hours to go check on our enemies.

When I finally exited my room, I was careful to not bump into them. I spied out each time I reached a corner and tiptoed slowly so the floor wouldn't creak. As I suspected, they were in the kitchen, making what looked like potions.

I felt bad about this. I didn't mean to leave them like that, to trick them, but I couldn't wait either. Though I also believed the dark witches wouldn't kill Sean and Shade until they had me, I knew they could torture them to the brink of death and back.

I couldn't bear that.

The front door was heavy and would probably have a telltale click when I opened it, so I slipped into the library and opened one of the big glass windows. After I crossed it to the porch, I didn't bother closing it. I knew I didn't have much time until the sisters found out I was gone.

The porch was extra squeaky, so I was careful where I stepped and how slow I went. But once I was free of that, I ran. I ran through the overgrown grass, right beside the long driveway, thinking that my steps would be muffled then.

At the edge of the property, I checked my phone.

I had called an uber to come pick me up at an intersection about half a mile from here. I had ten minutes to reach it before the appointed time. The uber driver had texted me right after I booked the drive, making sure I was asking him to come the right way. Poor man probably thought he would be mugged or killed.

I arrived at the spot two minutes before he did.

"Are you all right, miss?" the older man asked once I slipped into his car.

"Yes, sir," I said. He stared me, concern etched into his weary features. "I just ... I had a fight with my husband. He was ... violent. I want to go to my parents' house."

His eyes hardened. "Say no more, miss."

He stepped on the gas and drove us to New Orleans.

KNOWING THE DRIVER WOULDN'T LET ME STEP OUT FROM THE car in the middle of a dark elementary school parking lot, I searched the maps for a house or an apartment building nearby. I found a rundown subdivision behind the school, so I gave the driver that address.

I made him stop in front of a house, then waved at him as I made my way to the driveway. I had told him I would enter through a side door, so he wouldn't see me getting in the house and didn't need to wait for me.

I rounded the corner of the house, and as suspected, there weren't any side doors. He wouldn't know that either. I spied out and sure enough, the driver was still in front of the house. After about five minutes, he drove away. He had probably stayed because he was worried about me, about where I was going at this time of the night. What a kind soul.

Once he drove away, I marched away from the house to the school. The streets were quiet and dark. A chill ran down my spine. I knew this wasn't wise, but I had to do it. I couldn't leave Sean and Shade to their fates.

I walked into the empty parking lot beside the abandoned school—it always shocked how much abandoned real estate was in this country.

I stood right in the center and glanced at my phone in my hand.

Ten, nine, eight ...

Midnight.

Grace and Starla appeared from the darkness, as if they had poofed from thin air. Grace had her green snake coiled around her shoulders.

They halted about ten feet from me and looked me up and down.

"I didn't like the change in time," Starla said.

"That's what I could do," was all I said. I didn't know how much she and the others knew. Did she really know I was Arianna, or were they suspicious? What about Anna and Britta? Who knew the sisters were alive and well? Better to stay quiet about some things. "Where're Sean and Shade?"

Grace looked at me, and for a moment, I feared they hadn't even brought them here. That they had just lured me here.

Grace snapped her fingers. Five witches appeared from the darkness like she had a moment ago. Two held Sean's bound arms, one carried the small metal crate with Shade, and the other two stood behind them, probably there to make sure there was no problem.

My stomach clenched at the sight of them. Shade looked like an abandoned cat, and Sean ... oh, Sean. There were bruises on his face, and the ropes dug into the skin around his wrists. He dragged his feet and swayed to the sides as if he were drunk.

"They put up quite the fight," Grace said, sounding amused. "The familiar was easy to contain with the enchanted crate, but the human ... he was feisty."

"Every chance he got, he fought us." Starla glanced at Sean. "We had to sedate him."

Fury sparked inside of me, but I reined it in. It wasn't the time for that yet. "I'm here. Now let them go."

"Nah, that wasn't the deal," Starla said.

"The deal was that we wouldn't kill them if you came to see us," Grace explained. "As you can see, we haven't killed them."

I closed my hands into fists, my magic surging inside of me. "Let them go or—"

"Or what?" Grace snapped, sounding like a totally different person. Which shouldn't be a surprise. The bitch had tricked me from the beginning. "You're too weak to do anything to us."

I crossed my arms before I fried her alive with my lightning. That was what I wanted. To kill them all right here and right now, but despite the training this afternoon, I hadn't accessed and used one tenth of my power yet. I couldn't control it the way I should. What if I ended up hurting Sean or Shade? I couldn't risk it.

"What do you want?" I asked with a bravado I didn't have. "You wanted me to hear you, so say your piece."

Grace smiled at me, and I suppressed a shudder. Before, whenever she smiled at me, it had been sweet and warm. That lying snake had wrapped me around her finger with her charm. Now her smile was astute, knowing, almost wicked.

"By now you should know you're Arianna's reincarnation," she said, not one bit amused. I stayed quiet. "Arianna divided the dark and light witches because she thought all dark witches were evil. She was wrong, we aren't evil."

I snorted. "You look like it right now."

Starla groaned. "Just because some of us aren't kind and sweet all the time, doesn't mean we're evil."

"You were stealing ghosts from that haunted house!" I pointed at her. "What for? I still don't know what you do with those."

Grace glanced at her and nodded.

Starla went on, "I was working undercover, then. I had infiltrated a group of dark witches and they had sent me on an errand there. I had to prove myself to them." She gestured to me and Sean. "I think you two had tests where you had to do things you didn't think were right either."

I frowned. Was she joking?

"But it all worked out in the end, because Starla met you that night," Grace said. "And during your fight, she felt your magic."

I shrugged. "And?"

"My gift is to sense kinds of magic," Starla said. "The moment you struck me, I felt it. Only a sliver, hidden among the rest of your magic and the crystals' powers, and that ridiculous chicken bone the witch doctor gave you."

My mouth hung open. "How ... how do you know about that?"

"We know about a lot of things," Grace said, sounding like a queen.

"Anyway," Starla continued, "I felt the dark lightning mixed with the rest of your magic. I knew if you weren't Arianna's reincarnation, then you were somehow related to her." Arianna had died young with no children, but her sister had lived on and left the witching world behind, as far as we knew. "So, I let you defeat me. I let the Lightgrove witches take me because I had to know."

I gasped. "It was all on purpose?"

"Honestly, I thought you would have come to see me a lot sooner than you did, but it all worked out in the end."

"What worked out?"

Her lips stretched in a grin. "I'm free and you're here talking to us."

This was insane. "I still don't know what you want with me."

"We want you to take over the Lightgrove witches and united it with the Darkmist," Grace said. "We want you to restore the Lightmist coven and welcome all witches, light and dark, no exceptions."

My brows curled. "You're Darkmist witches. Who's your queen?"

Starla cleared her throat. "We left the Darkmist coven long ago."

"Why?" I couldn't help but ask.

"Because they were evil, and we're not."

"What do you call yourselves?"

"Ashmist," Grace said. "But we don't want it to stick, because we're hoping Lightmist will come back."

I thought for a second. "You said you left the Darkmist, but you want to reunite it with the Lightgrove? Why? Why not ask to join the Lightgrove, then?"

"Because the Lightgrove would never accept us," Starla said. "Our gifts are what was dubbed dark gifts. As for the Darkmist ... we believe most of its members aren't as evil as the queen would like them to be."

"Just like us," Grace said.

Could it be? Were they telling the truth? "I'm still not convinced. You hurt the Light Order when taking me out of the castle."

Grace shook her head. "I didn't hurt them. That spell was to scare them, to keep them busy, not to hurt them."

"Well, kidnapping Sean and Shade sure adds a point on the evil column."

Grace snapped her fingers again and the witches moved. The two holding Sean undid the ropes around his wrists, and the other one set the crate on the ground and opened the door.

Shade leapt from the crate and turned into his human form.

Sean stumbled forward and fell on his knees.

"Sean!" I started for him.

A strong wind blew me back. No, not just me. Everyone but Sean and Shade. A red rope of magic snaked past the wind, wrapped around Sean and Shade and pulled them back.

Then the wind died.

And I froze.

A dozen witches formed a line to my far left, their

clothes black. One witch held Shade in his cat form, and another one wearing a fancy black gown—clearly the ringleader—wrapped her hands around Sean's neck and pushed him down to his knees. A bat sat at her shoulder.

The ringleader grinned at me. "Hello, Hazel. Or should I say Arianna?"

12

___

I STARED AT THE NEWCOMERS AT A LOSS.

"Queen Catarina," Grace whispered. She, Starla, and the others took several steps back.

Oh, shit. Was this the queen of the Darkmist witches? The real evil bitch Grace was warning me about?

"Imagine my surprise when I found out about this little meeting." Queen Catarina looked from me to Grace. "I knew you had left us for ridiculous reasons, but ... for this?" She gestured her hand to me. "For her? That's pathetic."

Fear coiled around my muscles, but I had come this far. I stood tall and faced the queen of the dark witches. "Let Sean and Shade go."

She tilted her head. "Or what?"

I shifted my weight. "Or ... you'll regret it."

Catarina's head tipped back, and she let out a cackle worthy of a good horror movie. "From what I heard, you're weak, Hazel, without your full powers. You can't fight me."

"She's right," Starla whispered to me. "She's too strong. If you go head-to-head with her, she'll kill you."

I glanced at her. Back in the Light Castle's dungeon, I had thought Starla was the crazy one. Now I knew I had been wrong. She had pretended to get to me, and the real crazy one was Catarina, the wicked witch of the west who had her hands around Sean's throat.

"What do you want?" I asked her.

"Oh, nothing much." She ran her nails across Sean's skin. His head lolled back. The effect from the sedative was still strong in his system. "The same thing everyone seems to want these days ... a piece of the founder of the Light-grove coven."

The bat on her shoulder flew up and in that moment of distraction, she acted. She extended her hand and threw a black bolt at me. I yelped and jumped to the side. I landed hard on my foot and twisted my ankle. I fell to the ground and pain jolted through my hips.

A battle started. The Darkmist witches advanced and the Ashmist faced them halfway. I pushed up, pain ricocheting through me but determined to enter this damn fight and free Sean and Shade.

From across the parking lot, I saw as the witch holding Shade electrocuted him and threw him aside. He didn't get up. Then Queen Catarina put her hand on the top of Sean's head and dark magic enveloped him.

"No!" I cried. I started racing there, but with my twisted ankle and my hurt hip, I felt like a snail.

The dark magic seeped through his pores, his eyes, his mouth, his ears. He groaned, closed his eyes ... and then took a deep breath. Head low, Sean stood and pulled his hands apart, the rope breaking as if it was a thin elastic band.

Then he lifted his head and looked at me. I skidded to a stop, my heart skipping a beat.

His eyes were all black, dark lines crisscrossed his handsome face, his skin was paler than before, and he offered a smirk that chilled my bones.

"Sean," I whispered.

"Hello, Hazel," he said, his voice deeper than before.

I looked at the queen, who stood a couple of steps behind him, smiling and proud of her work. "What have you done?"

She lifted one shoulder. "I gave him a little bit of darkness. That darkness suppressed the good in him, and now he's evil."

No!

He ran his thumb over his lower lips. "What's the problem, Hazel? Don't you like the new me?"

I stared at him, stunned.

A bolt of magic zoomed past me, one inch from my nose, and I jumped back, suddenly aware of the fight going on around us.

I ducked and remained crouched, as if the others couldn't see me like this. I had to think, I had to think ... but my mind was a jumble, no thought made sense. All I could do was feel.

Oh my God, what had they done to Sean? And Shade? What had I done?

Stray magic kept flying my way and then they changed.

First, they came at my feet, forcing me to stand and push back. Then they came straight at me.

"Fight!" Queen Catarina said. "Hit me!" She threw bolt after bolt.

I spun around, avoiding one of them while calling my magic. She wanted a fight? I would give her a damn fight. Magic crackled around my fingers, and—

Grace jumped in front of me, her arms spread out.

Then her body slacked over me, her eyes wide.

"Run," she whispered, before falling to the ground at my feet.

A battle cry sounded in the distance and Starla rushed to the queen, engaging her directly.

Hands shaking, shallow breath, I glanced at Grace—there was a huge hole in her back, the edges charred.

If she hadn't thrown herself in front of me, that would have been my chest.

"Hazel." His voice startled me.

Sean was five feet from me, watching me with those demon-black eyes, a lopsided grin on his dark lips. Even his hair was darker now.

I gulped and took a step back. "You're not Sean."

"But I am," he said, stalking closer.

I wanted to run, I wanted to throw some distracting magic at him and run, but if this Sean was anything like mine, I wouldn't get three steps away before he caught up with me.

Still, I couldn't help it. I took another step back. "No. You'll never be."

With his long legs, he erased the distance between us

in two seconds, and I gasped when he loomed over me. His hand wrapped around my wrist, and he tugged me to him, his touch cold.

I held my breath, afraid to move.

"I am the same, Hazel." He blinked and the black taking over his eyes retreated until they covered only the irises. "My boring parts are gone, and the fun ones remained." He put my hand over his heart and leaned over me. "You can be like that too, and together, we would have so much fun."

He stared into my eyes, and I felt like crying.

This wasn't my Sean, doesn't matter what he said about it. My Sean was either gone or lost inside of this demon, and I had no idea what to do to bring him back.

"Sean," I whispered, pleading, as if the real Sean could hear me. "Please."

A blue bolt zipped past Sean's head and he turned toward it with a growl.

I sighed in relief as Anna and Britta ran to us, magic visible at their fingertips.

"Step away from her," Britta said, throwing another bolt.

To avoid being hit in the face, Sean released me and stepped back. I ran to meet the sisters.

"You stupid girl," Anna said, through gritted teeth. She and Britta touched my arms and shoulders, as if wanting to make sure I was okay, but pushed me behind them and faced the mess in front of us.

Sean stayed put and stared at us—at me—with sparkling eyes. The Darkmist witches still battled some of

Grace's witches, and a little farther away, Queen Catarina cast a spell that rendered Starla immobile.

The queen touched Starla's cheek as if caressing her, and magic rippled over her, and she gagged. A moment later, the magic holding her up faded and she slumped to the ground.

Dead.

The queen turned her attention to us.

"Oh, shit," Britta muttered. "Time to go." She swept her hand wide in front of her and Shade's crate zipped through the air and straight into her arms. "Now."

Anna grabbed my arm, and the sisters pulled me away from the parking lot, from the school.

And I let them take me.

But I couldn't help glancing back over my shoulder once and meeting Sean's eyes.

His lopsided grin taunted me. "We'll meet again, my love."

Continue reading Hazel's adventures with book 5, *The Midnight Hunt!*

BONUS: want to read an exclusive scene from Sean's POV? Download it here!

To read a special and exclusive book about another light witch, join my Facebook Group and find the book called *The Light Witch* to download on the "featured" tab!

THANK YOU

Thank you for reading *The Midnight Secret*!

Reviews are very important for authors. If you liked my book, please consider leaving a review on your favorite online retailer and/or on Goodreads and/or Bookbub, please!

Did you like this book? You can check out other books of mine:

The Night Calling (Rite World: Night Wolves book 1): she was abandoned by her mate, left in the hands of a terrible half-demon ... but now he's back and ready to claim her.

The Darkest Vampire (Rite World: Vampire Wars book 1): a witch releases a dark vampire from a curse, and becomes inadvertently bonded to him.

The Demon Kiss (Rite World: Blackthorn Hunters Academy book 1): a fast-paced story about a young woman who finds out she's a demon hunter, and the half-demon intent on protecting her against all evil.

The Vampire Heir (Rite World 1: Rite of the Vampire): a dark and mysterious paranormal romance about a vampire and a young woman with a secret.

The Warlock Lord (Rite World 4: Rite of the Warlock): a thrilling and kick-ass paranormal romance about a werewolf and warlock.

The Wolf Forsaken (Rite World 7: Rite of the Wolf): a heat-wrenching tale about a lost wolf shifter and a fae princess on the run.

Heart Seeker (The Fire Heart Chronicles book 1): an urban fantasy series about a young woman who finds herself at the center of a mysterious supernatural world.

Destiny Gift (The Everlast Series book 1): a post-apocalyptic urban fantasy series about a young woman with a special power that can save the world.

DON'T FORGET TO SIGN UP FOR MY NEWSLETTER TO FIND OUT about new releases, cover reveals, giveaways, and more!

If you want to see exclusive teasers, help me decide on covers, read excerpts, talk about books, etc, join my reader group on Facebook: Juliana's Club!

ABOUT THE AUTHOR

While USA Today Bestselling Author Juliana Haygert dreams of being Wonder Woman, Buffy, or a blood elf shadow priest, she settles for the less exciting—but equally gratifying—life as a wife, a mother, and an author. She resides in North Carolina and spends her days writing about kick-ass heroines and the heroes who drive them crazy.

Subscribe to her mailing list to receive emails of announcement, events, and other fun stuff related to her writing and her books: www.bit.ly/JuHNL

For more information:
www.julianahaygert.com

facebook.com/julianahaygert

twitter.com/julianahaygert

instagram.com/juliana.haygert

goodreads.com/juliana_haygert

pinterest.com/julianahaygert

bookbub.com/authors/juliana-haygert

youtube.com/julianahaygert

tiktok.com/@julianahaygert

ALSO BY JULIANA HAYGERT

To find links and more info, go to:
www.julianahaygert.com/books/

<u>Shorts</u>
Into the Darkest Fire

<u>Standalones</u>
Daughter of Darkness

<u>Rite World: Night Wolves</u>
The Night Calling (Book 1)
The Night Burning (Book 2)
The Night Hunting (Book 3)
The Night Rising (Book 4)

<u>Rite World: Vampire Wars</u>
The Darkest Vampire (Book 1)
The Darkest Witch (Book 2)
The Darkest Magic (Book 3)

<u>Rite World: Lightgrove Witches</u>
The Midnight Test (Book 1)
The Midnight Spell (Book 2)
The Midnight Flame (Book 3)
The Midnight Secret (Book 4)
The Midnight Hunt (Book 5)

<u>Rite World: Blackthorn Hunters Academy</u>
The Demon Kiss (Book 1)
The Hunter Secret (Book 2)

The Soul Bond (Book 3)
The Shadow Trials (Book 4)
The Infernal Curse (Book 5)

Rite World
The Vampire Heir (Book 1)
The Witch Queen (Book 2)
The Immortal Vow (Book 3)
The Warlock Lord (Book 4)
The Wolf Consort (Book 5)
The Crystal Rose (Book 6)
The Wolf Forsaken (Book 7)
The Fae Bound (Book 8)
The Blood Pact (Book 9)

The Wyth Courts
Winter King (Book 1)
Spring Warrior (Book 2)
Summer Prince (Book 3)
Autumn Rebel (Book 4)

The Fire Heart Chronicles
Heart Seeker (Book 1)
Flame Caster (Book 2)
Earth Shaker (Book 2.5)
Sorrow Bringer (Book 3)
Soul Wanderer (Book 4)
Fate Summoner (Book 5)
War Maiden (Book 6)

The Everlast Series
Destiny Gift (Book 1)
Soul Oath (Book 2)
Cup of Life (Book 3)
Everlasting Circle (Book 4)

Willow Harbor Series

Hunter's Revenge (Book 3)
Siren's Song (Book 5)

Breaking Series
Breaking Free (Book 1)
Breaking Away (Book 2)
Breaking Through (Book 3)
Breaking Down (Book 4)